# Victimized In Venice

## The House Sitters Cozy Mysteries

## Book 3

### SCARLETT MOSS

Abby Moss Publishing

Victimized in Venice, The House Sitters Cozy Mysteries Book Three- Scarlett Braden

Copyright © 2020 Scarlett Braden

All rights reserved. Printed in the United States of America. No part of this book may be used or reproduced in any manner whatsoever without written permission except in the case of brief quotations embodied in critical articles or reviews.

For information contact :
Scarlett Braden at ScarlettBraden@gmail.com

The scanning, uploading and distribution of this book via the Internet or any other means without the permission of the publisher is illegal and punishable by law. Please purchase only authorized electronic or physical editions, and do not participate in or encourage electronic piracy of copyrighted materials. Your support of the author's rights is appreciated.

This is a work of fiction. Names, characters, places, and incidents either are the product of the author's imagination or are used fictitiously, and any resemblance to actual persons, living or dead, business establishments, events, or locales is entirely coincidental.

# Chapter One

"HAVE YOU LOST YOUR MIND, Dad?" Kaylee Roberts said to her father. "That woman is behind this, isn't she?"

"Yes. It's an age-old truth. Women do cause men to lose their minds, be it their wives or daughters. There are songs, poetry, and literature extolling the dangers of females. Why in particular are you denigrating my wife today, Kaylee?" Ray Roberts asked.

"Holly just told me you have house-sitters coming to stay with Carina while you're in California. I don't understand how you can trust your home and that precious dog to strangers when you have family, right here in town. I could have stayed with Carina. Why didn't you even ask me?"

"Well, let's see. You have your apartment to look after. If you were here, who would take care of your place? Secondly, you are trying to run a business and you're working all the time. At least, that's what you tell us when we invite you to spend time with us. So where would that leave poor Carina? She needs to be walked several times a day. And fed. And played with."

"I just think it's weird that you're letting strangers stay in your house. It's just creepy. What do you even know about them? Please tell me you have better sense than to hire a local. Geez, Dad. I could have used the money. You should have asked me."

"We aren't paying money. No, it's not a local, not that there is anything wrong with a Venetian. But this is a program where people care for your pet and your home for free. And we know enough about them. They've passed thorough background checks. He is a retired sheriff from Texas. Holly has talked to them on the phone and likes them. Everything will be fine."

"I'm just saying, that's absurdly weird. People come to stay in your house for free, and you expect the artwork and silver to be here when you get back?"

"Kaylee, what in the world has made you so cynical? You've led a charmed life. You've never been a victim. Why are you so suspicious of people? You need to relax or you'll die an early death."

"Whatever, Dad. I was a victim. My mother threw me away. She didn't want me."

"And because of that, you got to live with us here in Italy. Something young women all over America would give anything to do."

"Yeah. Lovely Italy. Do you want me to check in over here from time to time and make sure everything is okay?"

"No. Please don't. Zach will be available for them if they need anything. Just leave them be, Kaylee. I mean it. They're here for a vacation. They're excited about experiencing Carnival. Carina will be fine. This couple has excellent references. It's going to be a super busy time for your tour company. The city will be bursting at the seams. Take care of yourself and your business. Leave mine to me, please."

"Fine, I'll see you when you get back then. I'll help with the post-theft inventory."

Once Kaylee was safe in the elevator, Holly came out of the kitchen from where she heard the entire exchange and approached her husband. She wrapped her arms around his neck.

## Victimized in Venice

"Well, that went about as expected. I'm sorry, I know you don't like upsetting her. But at least she didn't find out about dinner tonight," Holly said compassionately.

"You're right. I don't like upsetting her. But she's turning into a spoiled brat. She's twenty years old. I'm sure it does still hurt that her mother sent her away. But honestly, her behavior is what caused it. It's time she stops playing the victim card and owns her actions and consequences. I'm not sure where we went wrong, but as much as I don't want to upset her, I wouldn't leave Carina in her care. When we get back from this trip, I'm going to tell her I won't be bailing her out anymore. I don't trust her. What does it say that I trust strangers more than my daughter?"

"It says you're a wise man," she answered, kissed him, then said, "Come help me with dinner. They'll be here soon."

"We can't all have a perfect son like yours," Ray said sadly.

"I know. That's why I share him with you," she retorted.

~\*\*\*~

Alen and Joan Arny were on their third train in as many days. They had a few days to kill between their last house-sitting gig in London and this one in Venice. Though it would have been less expensive and much faster to fly, they opted to take the scenic route. Literally. A two-and-a-half-hour train ride took them to Paris, where they did a drive-by tour of the city. They hoped someday to land a house-sitting gig there to see more of the city, but at least they could say they'd seen the Eiffel Tower and the Louvre museum. The next morning, they took the train from Paris to Turin, Italy. The longer ride through the countryside was scenic, but six hours of watching the landscapes out the window gave Joan a stiff neck. With a shorter three-and-a-half-hour trip to Venice, they took the morning to have a leisurely breakfast of croissants, fruit, and coffee and walked the beautiful plazas of Turin with the Alps overlooking their shoulders. The weather was chilly, but they enjoyed the chance to walk. At noon, they headed to the train station for the final leg of the trip. Their excitement was building.

"I can't believe we're going to get to be in Venice for Carnival and Valentine's Day. Oh, Honey, this will be our most romantic Valentine's in our eighteen years together," Joan cooed. Both her arms were wrapped around his one as they sat snuggled together on the train waiting to depart the station.

"You know what I can't believe? We escaped Scotland without getting arrested. We made it out of England without getting arrested, although it was a close and scary call on a couple of occasions. We managed to travel in and out of France, with no one the wiser and no bodies turning up. And now, we're in Italy. I have a good feeling about this --" Alen said with a perfectly straight face. But before he could finish Joan had untangled her arms from around his and slugged him in the same arm.

"Alen!" she whispered. "Stop it. Why do you think this is funny? You just love to have everyone on the train looking at us and imagining that we've done the worst. You, a former sheriff, should know better than anyone that murder isn't funny!"

"I was just going to say I have a good feeling about Venice. It's the city of love. Romance. Fun. Games. Frivolity. No reason for murder, right? I even checked their crime statistics. Venice is safer than 71% of U.S. cities. Pickpocketing is their biggest crime, and that's to be expected in a high tourist area," Alen told her.

"Yeah, speaking of tourists, while we're here at the most romantic time, it's also the most crowded time. We have a few days here before the city gets even more crowded. I thought we should do the big tourist sites before the extra Carnival crowd shows up. What do you think?"

"Sounds good to me, I found several cooking classes I want to take. Pasta, pizza, pastries, oh my. We should coordinate the schedule. Most of them are only two to three hours, which gives us time for sightseeing too," Alen answered.

"Yeah, I saw some walking photography tours I think I will enjoy. I can do those while you're cooking. As always, I support these cooking classes above all else. After Venice, you'll have a nice repertoire of dishes you can woo your wife with," Joan teased.

"Speaking of repertoire, you're not planning to drag me to an opera, are you?" Alen asked apprehensively.

"Nope. Not me. I like to sing along to music, which means I need to understand the words. You're safe with me, handsome," she said.

"I got my Where-You-Traveled-This-Month email and map this morning from Google. Thankfully, it doesn't show a related body-count. I'm hoping that this is one stop on our travels where we don't meet the local police. It's fine with me to remain anonymous," Alen said quietly to avoid more physical abuse from Joan.

They both took out their phones and synchronized their schedule for the two weeks they would be in Venice, dog-sitting with Carina, the bulldog. Joan had read that Venice was very dog-friendly and they could take Carina with them almost everywhere they went. She was looking forward to it. Each of them silently prayed that this time they could just be visiting tourists with nothing more important to do than learn local recipes and take stunning travel photos.

SCARLETT MOSS

## Chapter Two

AT THE TRAIN STATION, THEY hired a water taxi to take them and their luggage to the home of Holly and Ray Roberts. In their suitcases were all their belongings in the world. They had retired from their jobs as sheriff and 911 dispatch operator, sold their home, car, and all their belongings in Corpus Christ, Texas, to become international house sitters. Kaylee Roberts had nothing to worry about. There was no spare room in the luggage for anything as frivolous as family silver or artwork.

Following the directions Holly had given them, they arrived at the building on the Fondamente Cannaregio, just a few buildings away from the Ponte Guglie on the Rio di Cannaregio and disembarked from the water taxi. They entered the gorgeous building and spoke to the guard. He showed them to an elevator, took out a key and set the elevator's destination to the Penthouse. The elevator smoothly and silently carried them to the fifth floor that would be home for them for the next two weeks. Joan and Alen were both remembering the jerky, creaky, elevator they were in last in London. The elevator opened to the smells of garlic and home cooking. They heard laughter and giggles. It sounded like a home.

Ray and Holly were standing at the elevator waiting to greet them and help them with luggage.

"Welcome to Venice!" Holly said hugging Joan.

Ray shook Alen's hand and said, "I hope you had an easy trip."

"We did, thank you," Alen answered back.

"Come in, we'll give you a tour," Holly said, grabbing one of Joan's suitcases.

The penthouse was a unique house in Venice. Most buildings were building-locked on at least two sides and usually three. Meaning many houses only had windows on one side. Joan had begun looking at houses and real estate online at each of their destinations. Her impression of most homes in Venice was that they were dark. But not this house. This building was taller than the building on the right of them and behind them, so the Penthouse had windows on three sides. It was open and had an airy feeling.

Holly gave them a tour of the three-bedroom penthouse. The décor was modern, not overly done like many Venice houses Joan looked at online. The other unique thing about this house was every available space in each room was filled with bookcases. Bookcases filled to overflowing with books. One of the spare bedrooms even featured a bookcase bed frame – the mattress and box springs rested upon a twelve-inch-tall bookcase with books underneath around the three exposed sides of the bed.

Back in the living room, Holly made the introductions to the rest of the family members there to meet Alen and Joan.

"This is my son, Zach and his wife, Lesley. These two precious little grand darlings are Avery and Brenna," Holly said introducing them.

"Nice to meet you all," Joan said.

The older of the two little girls approached Alen.

"I'm Avery. I'm first. That's why my name starts with A. I'm four years old. You're first too because your name starts with A. How old are you?"

The room erupted in laughter. Lesley called her daughter back, embarrassed.

"I'm sorry," she apologized to Alen, before turning to whisper in her daughter's ear that it isn't polite to ask adults how old they are.

"It's quite alright," Alen started to say, but Joan grabbed his hand, squeezed, and slightly, almost imperceptibly, shook her head no at him. He realized that he would be unteaching the lesson, Lesley was trying to teach her daughter if he answered.

Holly had walked over to a chair, set so that its occupant could see out the window as she rested.

"This is the excitable Carina. As you can see, she isn't bothered by children or company. She sits here most of the day, hoping to spy a cat walking along the roof edge of the building across the way It's about the only thing that excites the bella anymore," Holly explained.

Joan kneeled to scratch behind Carina's ears.

"Is she elderly?" Joan asked.

"Nope. She's just lazy. She's only three years old," Ray answered.

"She's not lazy!" Holly argued, "She's a regal lady, with decorum," she teased.

"It smells divine in here," Alen said.

"Dinner will be ready in just a moment. Lesley, will you help me get dinner on the table?" Holly asked.

"I can help," Joan said.

"No, no. Have a seat. Or, before it gets dark, Ray can point to some interesting neighborhood spots out the windows for you. Tomorrow, we'll show you around the neighborhood.

Usually, the first-night dinners with the homeowners for Alen and Joan had been filled with questions about them. What they did before, where they were from and what made them decide to be house sitters was usually the dinner conversation. But this night was more about the homeowners and their children.

While they enjoyed what Holly called Spaghetti Limoncello, a green salad, and a loaf of fresh herbed focaccia bread, they chatted around the table.

"We invited Zach and Lesley so you could meet them before we leave. They are both fluent in Italian, so if for any reason you have a problem and need an Italian speaker, you can call them," Ray explained.

"Do you have pets?" Joan asked Lesley.

"No, just the children," she said and they laughed.

"But you didn't want to house-sit?" Alen asked.

"No, we don't live in Venice. We live in Padua. But I work in Venice and am here in the daytime. Padua is only about forty-five minutes away. And it's also easier with the girls for them to be home," Zach answered.

"Oh. What do you do?" Joan asked Zach.

"Zach is trying to reverse the housing crisis for Venetians," Holly said proudly.

"The housing crisis?" Alen asked.

"Overtourism is taking a toll on the city. Not to mention the increased days of flooding too. Venice's population has dropped to between 53,000 and 55,000 permanent residents. But 20 million people a year visit the city. Some days, especially during Carnival, we might have two million people in the city. Between foreigners moving into the city, buying property and paying more than a local can and people converting homes into vacation rentals, a housing shortage has resulted, which then leads to higher prices. Statistics have shown us that two Venetians move out of the city every day because they can't find affordable housing. And an agency I work with says six Venetians are evicted every day," Zach explained.

"Zach is an architect and civil engineer with a doctorate in urban planning," Lesley told them.

"Holy cow, that's terrible!" Joan exclaimed.

"On top of all that, the city is billions of dollars in debt. The city owns a lot of housing, but it's fallen into disrepair and instead of spending the money to fix things, they shutter the houses and they sit empty. We try to find those empty houses and restore them to make them available to local people needing housing," Zach explained.

"How do you finance the projects?" Alen asked, interested.

"I have a Patreon account. People make small monthly contributions. We do as much as we can. There are some large palazzos up for sale by the state to raise funds to decrease debt. If I could raise enough money to buy one or two of them, we could convert them into apartments and make a significant difference for the people here," Zach explained.

"So, in other words, you're working with the city to rehabilitate the houses?" Alen asked.

"No, not really. I don't want to say the city doesn't care, though I'm sure it feels that way to people who are desperate for a place to live. The city has no funds to do anything about it. That's one of the reasons they are going to implement a new entry fee to the city later this year. I understand urban planning. What I don't understand is why the city is so in debt. I guess the entry fee is supposed to help reduce that debt. But that doesn't help people in the meantime," Zach answered.

"Well, then how do you find these houses to renovate? And are you saying you're doing these renovations without the permission or knowledge of the city?" Joan asked.

"Technically, we're squatting. We find these abandoned apartments through word of mouth. People don't like abandoned places in their buildings or neighborhoods. They attract pests, decrease property values, make buildings harder to heat in the winter. All the same things as back in the U.S. that make abandoned homes undesirable. Venice is a small town like any other and word travels fast. So, the locals tell us when they find an abandoned place. We do a property search. If it's owned by the city, we just quietly take over. I think they know we're doing it, and they turn a blind eye. We then charge a reasonable rent for the apartment or house, and that money goes into the coffers to do more," Zach explained.

"Wow, what a project!" Alen said. "The people who donate to your Patreon, are they mostly locals?"

"No, actually they are not. I went to undergrad in the U.S. but got both my master's degrees here in Italy. Then I went back to the U.S. for my doctorate. By then, Mom and Ray were living here, and Mom was telling me about the issues. I started the Patreon account. Most of my donations come from the United States, some from other parts of Italy, and a few from other places around the world who have heard about our project. A German reporter did a documentary about the housing crisis here and in the process learned about our project. We got a few subscribers from around Europe too," Zach told them.

"We want to subscribe!" Joan said.

"Yes, give us the info before you go," Alen said.

"Thanks! It's been great visiting with you. But we need to get our sleepy-headed girls home before they get wound up and cranky," Lesley said.

They all said good night, and then Alen and Ray took Carina for her nightly walk while Joan helped Holly with the dishes and dinner cleanup.

# Chapter Three

SATURDAY MORNING, FOLLOWING COFFEE, THE two couples took off together for Carina's morning walk at 7:30 a.m.

They crossed over the Ponte delle Guglie, the gargoyle bridge, to the side of the canal that would take them into the heart of Venice.

Ray explained that the Carnival parades that took place on the Grand Canal would end here on the Rio del Cannaregio and that Cannaregio was the name of their area of town. This area was originally known as the Jewish Ghetto. Alen and Joan noticed a lot of boat traffic already on the canal but not gondolas or the water taxi like they took to the Roberts' penthouse from the train station. Holly explained that these were supply boats used to restock stores and restaurants before they opened. She also told them that a water taxi or bus was called *vaporetto* and the ferry that simply took you from one side of the canal to the other when there wasn't a nearby bridge was called a *traghetto*.

Down an alley just past the bridge were tents that would open soon and was a produce market. Alen and Joan were thrilled with the easy walk to buy produce as they were realizing how complicated life could get in the city on water. Just a few more blocks away and they reached their first doggie pit stop of the day, a big green park with lots of trees and walking paths called Parco Savorgnan.

"This is usually our first stop of the morning," Holly explained. "And then we go about our business around the city. We don't have very many green spaces here in the city, and the dogs have to get accustomed to going on the concrete. Carina thinks she's too good for that. But if we don't make it to the park, she'll go whereever she has to," Holly told them.

"Yeah, watch your step, especially in the plazas. Not everyone is good about picking up after the little poop machines," Ray said.

"Ray!" Holly admonished. "Don't call the four-leggeds names. It's not nice. They can't help it that getting on a toilet is a challenge for them," she teased.

"We were talking before we fell asleep last night about how impressive Zach and Lesley are. You must be proud of him," Joan said.

"We are," Ray answered. "I just wish we could be as proud of my daughter. Between us, we have one child working passionately to save the people of this city and the other all but hates this place, especially the people," he said sadly.

"You have another child here?" Alen asked.

"Yeah, my daughter. She's twenty. We've told her not to come around while we're gone. If she shows up and the guard calls you, just tell him you aren't accepting guests," Ray said.

"If she's unhappy here, why does she live here?" Joan asked confused.

"She came to live with us when she was sixteen," Holly explained. "She's been a handful ever since. She strongly dislikes Italy. She hasn't even attempted to learn the language but then gets frustrated when she can't communicate. A lot of people here, at least those that deal with the tourists, speak at least enough to get them through their service jobs. But also, all the tourists who come here don't speak English. They come from all over the world and speak every language," Holly explained as they walked.

"Pardon me," Ray said, "That's where we buy meat," he said pointing across the alley they were walking. "And around the corner is the hardware store, but you shouldn't need that while we're gone. Seriously, if you need anything at all, just call Zach."

"Won't your daughter feel abandoned with you gone?" Joan asked.

"Her name is Kaylee. And no. She has her own life. She started a tour company and has about eight employees she manages. She has friends. We rarely see her. And if she has a crisis, she can call Zach. For sure I don't understand it, because they are so different, but the boy adores and dotes on his step-sister. Even though they are step-siblings, they call each other brother and sister and are as close as any natural siblings. She'll be fine and shouldn't need anything from you or our house while we're gone."

"How did you guys come to live in Venice?" Alen asked.

"I work for Amazon and Holly works for Google. A few years ago, Amazon wanted to open up in Italy, and I volunteered to be a project manager. Holly talked Google into sending her over to oversee the street view project. After a couple of years, we were set and could work from virtually anywhere. We had both fallen in love with Venice on a weekend trip and decided to move here. We bought the penthouse before we knew what a shamble the ex-pats and tourists had caused to the housing industry here. That's why Zach lives in Padua. He refuses to contribute to the problem," Ray told them.

"And Kaylee? Where does she live?" Joan asked.

"Well, that's where I'm a failure as a parent," Ray answered. "She lives in an apartment here on the island. I help pay her rent. She doesn't even have a roommate, like most people her age need here. Honestly, her friends are all from the U.S. and the U.K. and are part of the problem along with her."

"Did you have plans for the day?" Holly asked.

"I was thrilled to find the self-guided tours here. They are not only much more affordable than the guided tours, I like the go-at-your-pace option. Isn't technology neat, that our phone will use GPS to know where we are and then we can listen to a recorded bit about the sights? Anyway, we usually start in a new place with a general walking tour to give us a basic understanding. We can do that today or we can wait until tomorrow. Whatever you need us to do," Joan explained.

"We still need to finish up some work and pack before we leave. Our flight leaves at 7:30 a.m. tomorrow. I thought we could get pizza for dinner from our local pizzeria. Or what the Venetians do is bar hop among the *bacari*, or wine bars and eat *cicchetti* or appetizers for dinner. We have several in the neighborhood we can show you if you prefer."

"Either one sounds great. We will continue with our tour. I want to see San Marco Plaza before the city fills up with Carnival tourists," Joan said.

They parted ways. Ray, Holly, and Carina headed home, while Joan and Alen followed Ray's directions to get to the tour's starting point.

Along the Venice introductory tour, Alen and Joan learned that the city was first inhabited by fishermen but in the $5^{th}$-century hordes of gothic barbarians were looting their way through Rome. Citizens escaped to the islands that form Venice for protection and created the city that still exists today.

The first stop on the tour was the Palazzo Ducale, or Doge's Palace. The Doge was the early ruler of the city, elected for life and supported by a council of ten members and a grand council of two thousand members. This method of government existed until the Napoleon invasion in 1797. The palace was also the home of the local prison. Its most famous inmate was Casanova, who was also the only prisoner to ever escape. The palace is in San Marco square. St. Mark the Evangelist, or San Marco, is the patron saint of Venice after being interred there in the $9^{th}$-century.

## Victimized in Venice

They learned that the San Marco Campanile is the bell tower on San Marco plaza and that from the top of the tower is where Galileo first demonstrated the telescope to the Doge of Venice in 1609. It's ninety-nine meters high and the tallest structure in Venice. They also learned that in 1902 the tower crumbled, the bell ringing on the way down to alert those enjoying coffee in the café below.

"Remind me not to drink coffee near this tower," Alen said.

Joan knew he was teasing. A place that Alen couldn't enjoy a cup of coffee didn't exist anywhere on Earth. And he demonstrated how well she knew him when he then offered a suggestion.

"Hey, I'm starving. We didn't eat breakfast. Look, there's a café. Let's get some breakfast and a coffee before we continue," he suggested.

"See, I knew this self-guided tour thing was a grand idea. I'm game. Let's go."

After spending over thirty euros for two cappuccinos and two brioche pastries, the couple vowed they wouldn't be eating in San Marco Piazza again. Joan had read it was the most expensive area of the city but didn't ever imagine they would pay that much for a piece of bread and coffee.

They continued their tour. The most fascinating story of the day was revealed when listening to the recording about how St. Mark's Basilica came to be. The saint was originally buried in Egypt, but two Venetian merchants stole the body and hid him in barrels of pork to bring back to Venice. They knew the Muslim guards wouldn't touch the barrels of pork. Legend tells that once Mark's body was brought to Venice, an angel appeared and said, "Peace be with you, Mark, my Evangelist. Here shall your body rest."

They continued on the tour and learned about the clock tower, the most famous meeting place in the city; the iconic Rialto Bridge; and the Rialto market. They stopped the tour and decided to do some shopping for groceries in the market.

"Sweetheart, I'm not sure why, but I feel wiped out. Can we finish the tour tomorrow?" Alen asked as they left the market.

"Sure. I planned to do the Basilica and Doge Palace tours tomorrow, but it's in the afternoon. We still have a lot of this tour left. There are churches, museums, art, and palaces left to see in the introduction. But I think the last few days on the train have us out of our walking routine. We can take a water taxi back and have a rest before dinner," she answered.

~***~

They decided with their hosts to just get pizza for dinner, and they talked about the city.

"I've heard that the majority of Carnival activities take place in San Marco Piazza," Joan said.

"That's true. People will be dressed up and putting on skits, singing, and performing all sorts of entertainment throughout the days. The problem is that so many people come, the police institute crowd control. If you don't arrive early in the morning, you will have to stand in a long line to get into the square, and you might not even get in at all. Of course, it's the craziest on the weekends," Ray explained.

"Are you guys excited about Carnival? Is it something you want to participate in?" Holly asked.

"I think it's fun and fascinating, but I've read that the costumes can cost hundreds of euros to rent for a day and that the balls and galas also are very expensive, and I imagine it's too late to get tickets. But I do hope to get lots of fun photographs," Joan said.

"Yeah. In Scotland, she took photos of every man she could find wearing a kilt and playing the bagpipes," Alen teased.

"Well, I was just thinking. Ray and I have enjoyed every year of Carnival since we've been here. It's one of our only extravagances, other than books, as I'm sure you've noticed, but every year we have costumes made. You guys are close enough in size to us that you could borrow a costume if you would like," Holly said.

"Really?" Joan asked, stunned. "You wouldn't mind?"

### Victimized in Venice

"Come on, let's have some fun! You might have to rent shoes, but I bet we can make the rest work," Holly said.

They spent the rest of the evening trying on costumes and accessories and then they all walked Carina for her evening walk together. Joan thought she could already feel the Carnival excitement in the atmosphere.

"I bought tickets to one of the balls before I knew we would have to go to this meeting in California. You're right, all the galas are sold out. But if you would use the tickets, you're welcome to them," Ray told them before they turned in for the night.

"Cool!" Alen said, surprising Joan more than anyone. When Alen saw the look on her face, he calmed, sobered, and said, "What? It's better than an opera!"

SCARLETT MOSS

# Chapter Four

IT WAS AN EARLY MORNING in the Roberts' penthouse as Holly and Ray left to catch their early morning flight. As the sun came up, Alen and Joan struck out for Carina's morning walk and a day in the city. They decided with Holly and Ray the day before to take Carina along as they explored to keep her mind off her traveling parents and being left behind.

After a walk around the park, they headed into the heart of the city to continue the tour from yesterday.

"I truly do like these self-guided tours. You said they are less expensive?" Alen asked as they walked.

"Yeah, five euros for the two of us. And they have all sorts of them. I like them too. We can take Carina with us, go at our own pace, and stop whenever we like. But we might not get to see all the places if we go too slow. Who knew there was so much to see? I always thought the city was mostly about the gondolas. I also didn't realize that Venice is a hundred and eighteen separate islands. The buildings are built on wooden platforms supported by wooden pillars sunk into the ground of the islands. That's why it's called a floating city," Joan told him.

"Saving money on tours is a great thing. I found several cooking classes, but they aren't inexpensive. It sounds like our entertainment allowance will balance out," Alen said.

"I'll gladly stay home in my pajamas and look at pictures of Venice on the internet if that's what we need to do for you to keep learning to cook!" she countered.

Following the directions of the tour on their phones and picking up where they left off the day before, they visited Santa Maria Gloriosa Dei Frari, a church; Scuola Grande di San Rocco, a religious fraternity that took decades to decorate; Campo Santa Margherita, the square where the young locals hang out surrounded by bars; Ca' Rezzonico – Museum of 18th-Century Venice; Gallerie dell' Accademia, the famous art academy. Upon which time, Alen made his famous declaration.

"I'm hungry," he said.

They found a delightful café with outdoor seating and decided to share a plate of the dish Venice is most famous for, *risotto al nero di sepia*, or squid ink risotto.

"It's a good thing we ate so many salads in England. All this pasta, bread, and pastries look and smell so good. If we aren't careful our clothes won't fit when we leave here," Joan said.

"That's why we shared lunch. So we can stop for some gelato. Ray told me Carina really likes gelato. She's been such a good dog I think she deserves a treat," Alen said.

"You mean that portion of ham we just gave her wasn't a treat?" Joan asked.

"Nope. That was lunch," Alen clarified.

"Honey, your mouth is all black!" Joan squealed when she looked at him.

"Yours is too," he told her. "I think coffee is just the thing to get rid of the ink."

## Victimized in Venice

"There must be some trick. That dish or some version of it is on every menu in town, and yet, people aren't walking around with black mouths," she complained.

"How about we finish the sights on the tour, we only have four more stops, then we reward ourselves with gelato?" Joan proposed.

Along the way, Joan noticed the blinking green cross outside a store. She knew that meant the business was a pharmacy. She ducked inside and asked about gum. She was told to go to the tobacco store around the corner. Alen and Carina happily followed her on her new mission. Sure enough, they found gum and all sorts of candy at the tobacco store. She chose a brand called Vivident with the hopes that chewing the gum would help clear away the black squid ink from their teeth and tongues. The gum did help a little, but the clerk in the tobacco store told her as soon as they brushed their teeth, the black would be all gone. Joan decided that, since they liked the flavor of the dish, they should carry toothbrushes and toothpaste with them.

They finished out the day having visited Palazzo Cavalli-Franchetti, a sixteenth-century palace that is now the headquarters of the Venetian Institute of Science, Letters, and Art and hosts contemporary art exhibits; Squero di San Trovaso, a shipyard for building and repairing gondolas; Palazzo Barbarigo, another sixteenth-century palace whose façade is a mural made of famous Murano glass; and the Peggy Guggenheim Collection of contemporary art.

"Sweetheart, I've changed my mind," Alen announced.

"Oh? You don't want gelato?" Joan asked surprised.

"Of course, I want gelato. I think Carina and I deserve a double treat after all that," he answered.

"What then? What did you change your mind about?" she asked.

"Opera is not the worst thing in Venice," he proclaimed.

"You're kidding me, right? This place is gorgeous and so full of history. What on earth could be worse than opera?"

"At least you can sit down at the opera. My feet are killing me. And my eyes are burning, I don't think architecture and elaborate decors are my things," he explained.

"Well, we promised we were going to do new things. We didn't say we would like them all," she reminded him.

"Don't they have any shady characters? Serial killers? I enjoyed the great mystery tours in Scotland and England. Are there not any rogue characters more interesting or controversial than glass factory owners ticking off the neighbors with glass murals on the front of their palaces?"

"Wow, you *are* crabby. Let's stop at this café. You need coffee. Hopefully, they have gelato too," she said.

Once coffee and gelato were ordered and they were sitting outside at a table with Carina, Joan decided to more accurately answer his question.

"As far as I know, Venice has no equivalent to Sherlock Holmes, Rip Van Winkle, or James Bond. They do claim Casanova, though. I'll try to find a tour about him. I haven't heard stories of a great fire or the Black Plague. But I'll look into it," she promised.

The waiter looked a bit confused as he approached the table with three dishes of gelato and two coffees.

"One is for Carina," Alen explained. But Joan didn't think the young man spoke English as he didn't seem to understand and set two of the dishes in front of Alen and one in front of Joan.

Alen reached down to set a bowl in front of Carina. Like magic, her nose hovered over the bowl and in an instant, before Alen's hand released the bowl, it was empty. They both laughed.

"Where did the gelato go?" Joan howled.

"Holy cow, she inhaled it!" Alen exclaimed.

They decided to take a water bus home, delighted that in Venice, dogs were welcome aboard.

Alen prepared dinner that night, tossing some of the fresh vegetables with spaghetti and making a salad. While he fixed dinner,

## Victimized in Venice

Joan pulled out the three items they took with them wherever they went to make the house feel more like home.

First, she placed the framed picture of them from their wedding day on the nightstand on Alen's side of the bed. Then she carried the quilted table runner with frogs on it that her coworkers gave her and his and her frog salt and pepper shakers Alen gave her for their first anniversary to the dining table. Joan had always collected frogs of every sort, and she sold her collection before leaving Texas. These, along with a charm bracelet full of frog charms Alen had given her through the years and a frog broach he gave her just before leaving Corpus Christi, were all the frogs she had left. The frogs on the table runner with frames in diamond shapes of primary-colored fabrics and between them, she had attached all of Alen's Marine emblems, badges, and ribbons from his career in the Corps. Now she declared the penthouse home until time to go to the next place.

After dinner, Joan went to look for something to read. Holly and Ray had told them to help themselves to the vast library spread out all through the house. She spent some time analyzing and finally figured out their library sorting system. She found mysteries in the third bedroom. She found a book by one of her favorite authors, C.A. Newsome, who wrote a mystery series about a dog park. She was thrilled to find the book was one she hadn't read yet called *Fur Boys*. And then she noticed something else. A photo of a beautiful young lady. She picked up the frame and looked at the photo. The girl staring back at her had to be Ray's daughter, Kaylee. She favored him too much for any other explanation.

When she returned to the living room, Alen was watching a YouTube video about Casanova and Carina was in her favorite chair, on her nightly stakeout of cat watching. She looked at Joan briefly before looking back out the window.

"If that dog could talk, I think she just told me that I caused her to miss the catwalk," Joan said.

"Yeah, I don't think she was impressed with your tour either," Alen said.

Joan ignored him and spent the evening reading a book.

# Chapter Five

ALEN AND JOAN DISCOVERED THEY loved the sunrise walks with Carina. The city was quiet, but the canal was bustling with the supply boats darting around and offloading. It didn't feel like the city was asleep, but there weren't many people walking around yet. The bridges weren't crowded. And usually by 8:00 a.m. they could find a café open with coffee and brioche for breakfast.

They discovered Venetians didn't sit down for a big breakfast like a full English breakfast or American breakfast. For Venetians, breakfast was coffee and pastry standing up at the counter or on the go walking.

"Maybe that's how they keep trim while eating all the fried sweets and pastries," Joan commented.

They walked toward the grand canal and turned west. They were walking toward the train station and the docks where the cruise ships docked. But Joan knew from an app on her phone that no ships were going to dock this day. Even as the hour grew later, this part of town didn't seem too busy. Joan walked closer to the canal with Alen and Carina on her right.

"Look, Alen. It's a duffel bag floating in the water. Should we pull it out?"

"I reckon we should. Maybe it will have identification tags and we can return it to the owner. The bag looks full," he commented.

Joan could just reach the handle on the end and grasped it. The bag was heavy.

"This bag is full, waterlogged, and heavy. It feels like a bag full of books. Or soaking wet clothes. I can't lift it out of the water. Can you help me?"

Alen dropped Carina's leash certain the chubby lazy little dog would not sprint away and tried to help Joan lift the duffel out of the water. They both strained with the weight of it, but finally got it to the edge of the walkway and dragged it up to the concrete.

"This feels more like gold bricks. Hey, maybe we have a mystery on our hands. As much as I've hated having our trips interrupted by solving mysteries, this is one time I would welcome it," Alen said while searching the bag for luggage tags. He didn't find one.

"Alen, you've enjoyed our tours everywhere else," Joan protested, still perplexed and trying to understand why Alen didn't like the tours.

"I know. But they were interesting to me. It wasn't just architecture and pretty things. It's fine. I'll still go on them with you. I just don't find them as entertaining as the ones we've taken before. Looking at buildings is just not my thing, I guess," he said. "I guess we need to open the bag up and see if we can find any identification inside," he said. "It's too heavy to take home with us, that's for sure."

He unzipped the bag, and they were horrified by what was inside.

It wasn't clothes or books or even gold bars. Inside the oversized duffel bag was a body. Joan gasped and turned away. Alen shook his head as he pulled his phone from his pocket and called the phone number that anywhere in the world would summon help.

On the scene, the police told them that this happened once before. They told a story of a woman who was killed and thrown overboard from one of the cruise ships and supply boat operators fished it out of the canal. In broken English, the officer who was talking with them told them those kinds of murders took a long time to solve with all the tourists who were in the city for just a day. Once they gave the officers their contact info, where they were staying and their story of house sitting, they were on their way back home.

They were both quiet on the way home. Despite helping to solve murders in both Scotland and England, today's was the first body Joan had discovered. The discovery was hard on both of them.

When they returned to the penthouse, Alen asked her, "What did you have planned for today?"

"I found an experience I thought you would like. There's a new Casanova Museum and Experience with a theatrical flair. Kind of like the London Dungeon we liked. I thought we could give it a try. But I'm not sure I'm in the mood, now," she answered.

"Okay, then. What would you like to do? How would you prefer to spend the day?" he asked.

"I don't know. It just seems wrong to go about being tourists when a young woman has lost her life. Her family and friends have lost a loved one," she answered, dropping herself onto the sofa with a heavy sigh.

"I hear you and I understand," he said compassionately. "But, if we sit here all day, we'll likely just sink further into depression. Luckily, that lady isn't someone we know. There isn't anything we can do to help. The situation is out of our hands. I think we should do something besides sitting here. But it's up to you."

"You're right. I know you are. And getting out will help push the tragedy out of our minds I suppose. How have you handled this situation in your years of being a sheriff?" she asked.

"Death is always hard. Nothing about finding a body gets any easier. At least this time, we don't have to be the ones to tell her loved ones she's gone. And the case doesn't involve us. We aren't responsible for finding out what happened to her. Being in a suitcase in an Italian canal doesn't exactly scream natural causes. The discovery will weigh heavily on us. We probably won't want to walk in that direction anymore. But we are going to be just fine, Sweetheart. I promise," and he hoped he was right. No one knew how something like that would affect them until they experienced it. More than a few law enforcement officers found they couldn't handle the trauma and left the profession after their first experience.

Joan got up from the sofa, sighed a heavy sigh again and said, "Let's go shake this off. I don't think that's going to happen, but at least maybe Casanova can take our mind off the tragedy for a while. Do you think we'll be able to find any news about the lady or what happened to her later?"

"I'm not sure, but we'll check when we get home," he told her.

They enjoyed the Casanova Museum and Experience. The museum was opulent and historical, which Joan enjoyed, and learning how the author, artist, and lover operated was interesting to Alen.

"That was very cool, Sweetheart," he told her as they were leaving. "Thank you for finding the opportunity for me. I hope you enjoyed the experience too."

"I did. It's pretty remarkable how he escaped from the Doge's prison, huh? And no one else ever has. Kinda makes me wonder if he didn't have an accomplice on the inside," she said.

"How about a pastry and a coffee before we go home? We didn't eat lunch," Alen pointed out.

"I'm sorry. I didn't feel like eating, but you didn't mention food either. Coffee and sweets sound good, now, though," she said as they began to watch for a café that would fill their needs.

## Victimized in Venice

"How are you feeling? Any better?" he asked her tenderly while firmly holding her hand as they navigated around the crowded walkways.

"It did take my mind off of finding the duffel bag a little bit. But I still feel heavy. And sad. What on earth could have possibly caused someone to do her harm?"

"In my experience, love, jealousy, and greed are usually the basest motives."

"The whole situation is extremely sad," she said.

"Maybe tiramisu and coffee will help," he said hopefully. Alen understood the flood of emotions she was going through. He was experiencing them too. He simply hated to see her distressed and sad.

When they returned home, they went together to take Carina on her evening walk. They both automatically turned in the opposite direction from their walk this morning. They decided to follow the Venetian tradition of stopping at the bars along the walk, ordering a glass of wine or a spritz, a prosecco and soda water cocktail, and a small plate of *cicchetti*, finger food appetizers, instead of dinner after their late afternoon snack. Mozzarella en Carozza, a fried mozzarella sandwich at one bar and some classic bruschetta at another satisfied them for the night.

Alen and Joan curled up together to watch a movie before taking Carina for her last walk of the day right before bedtime. They seemed to be recovering from the morning incident but needed to be close to one another. The house phone rang. Alen got up to answer it. He hung up and looked at Joan.

"Oh, brother. Here we go again," he sighed.

"What is it?" Joan asked. They could hear the elevator ascending.

"The police are here," he answered as the elevator door opened exposing two officers, one man and one lady officer, both in snappy dress navy uniforms.

Alen and Joan looked at each other. Alen could tell Joan wanted to say something but was holding her tongue.

*"Ciao, mi dispiace, non parlo Italiano. Parla Inglese?"* Joan asked. It was the only Italian she knew, but she had studied the phrase. The words meant, hello, I'm sorry I don't speak Italian, can you speak English?

"Si, I can speak a little English," the lady said. "I am Ispettore Capo Pula, and this is Ispettore Superiore Muni. We need to speak to Signore Roberts."

"Holly and Ray Roberts are out of the country," Alen said stepping forward. "We are house sitters here taking care of the dog. I'm Alen Arny, and this is my wife, Joan. Can we help you?"

"The dog? She does not bark or even greet a stranger?" Pula asked looking for the dog.

Carina was looking at them curiously at least, but she was still sitting in her designated chair.

"I am afraid you cannot help. Can you tell us how to reach him?" the senior inspector Muni asked.

"We only have an email address. But his son lives in Padua. We can call him if that would help," Alen said.

"Do you have an address for him in Padua?"

"No, signore. Only a telephone number," Alen explained.

"Then that will have to do. If you could give us his name and phone number, we will be on our way. We are sorry to bother you," Pula said.

Joan was already copying Zach's name and phone number off the list of information Holly left for them. She handed the piece of paper to Pula.

"Can we ask what this is regarding?" Joan asked.

"We cannot say. We need to speak directly to Signore Roberts. Maybe his son can help us connect to him," Pula said. They turned and left in the elevator.

## Victimized in Venice

Alen looked at Joan. "When they arrived, you looked like you wanted to say something. What was it?" he asked.

"You just had to hope for a mystery, some excitement, some adventure. Here you go. No more boring architecture," she said, teasing him. "But seriously, what do you think it could be about?"

"A prize-winning question, to be sure. I suppose we'll hear from Zach. If not, we can call him tomorrow and ask. Or not. We *could* assume it's none of our business and go on blissfully happy as if nothing was going on," Alen said.

"Really? You and I could act like the Polizia di Stato didn't just show up at 9 p.m. looking for the homeowners?"

"Nope. That won't happen. I just said it could happen," Alen said.

Carina finally descended from her chair and walked to the elevator an indication that she was decreeing it was time for her bedtime walk.

~***~

"Should we try to guess what's happening? Or place bets?" Joan asked as they walked arm in arm walking Carina.

"You mean like a tournament squares game where each square represents a different crime or police matter and we place wagers as to which crime it turns out to be?" Alen asked.

"That sounds fun. We could start doing that on the way to each destination," Joan said.

"I think gambling is illegal in Italy," Alen said.

"Um, Alen. We are currently walking past a casino," Joan said.

"So we are. We should add gambling debt to the list of possible concerns then?"

"Although it's not in my nature, I guess we'll just have to wait to hear from Zach. Or Ray and Holly."

# SCARLETT MOSS

## Chapter Six

FOLLOWING CARINA'S MORNING WALK, ALEN and Joan were preparing for their day.

Alen was attending a *cicchetti* cooking class and Joan was following along on a photo walk.

"Which apron should I wear to my class?" Alen asked.

He was holding up an apron Joan gave him for Christmas which was printed with a buff bare-chested man wearing only a kilt, and the one the homeowners in London brought him from the United States that said, "Not all superheroes wear capes, some wear aprons."

"Hmm, I always think the hunk suits you best," she answered.

"No, you just have a thing for kilts," he teased.

"Truth. I wonder what kind of apron you need from Italy," Joan wondered aloud.

"No more aprons. Suitcase space, remember," he reminded her.

"I know. But a girl can dream," she muttered. She finished packing her camera bag with spare battery and memory cards, and they prepared to leave together for their day apart.

Before they got to the elevator, the house telephone rang and they heard the elevator ascending.

"I'll get it," Alen said.

Alen answered the phone and thanked the caller. He hung up and turned to Joan.

"Zach is on his way up," and the elevator opened.

"I suppose our wait is over to see what the visit was about," she said.

Inside was a distraught man. He looked as if he hadn't slept in days. He looked physically ill.

"Zach, what's wrong?" Joan asked gently.

"Kaylee is dead," he blurted out before exiting the elevator.

"What?" Joan asked. I'm so sorry, what happened?"

Joan put an arm around the man and gently led him to the sofa and sat down with him. Alen went to the kitchen and came back with a glass of water for Zach. He sat down in a chair across from them and waited. They both knew Zach would speak when he was ready.

"The police called last night. They said you gave them my number. Thank you for that. They didn't even want to tell me what it was. They only wanted to speak to Ray. I was able to get him on the phone. He called the police and then called me back."

"We're here for you, Zach," Joan said. "What can we do to help?" She worked hard to keep from asking all the questions she wanted to ask.

"She was murdered. They found her in the canal. Some people saw a duffel bag and pulled it out of the river and called the police," Zach said almost trancelike.

Joan gasped and her hand automatically covered her mouth.

"Oh, no," Alen said. "Zach, we found her. We were the ones who called the police. But we didn't know she was Kaylee. We're so sorry. You said it was murder. Do they have any leads?"

"I don't think so. I don't know. All Ray was able to tell me was that she was strangled, crammed in that duffel bag and dropped in the canal," Zach said.

"Will Holly and Ray be returning now?" Joan asked.

"I'm not sure. Ray is calling Pamela, Kaylee's mother to determine what to do. We have to decide whether to bury her here or send her back to the States."

"Of course. We are happy to help any way we can. Did the police question you at all?" Alen asked.

"No. Just how to get in touch with her father," Zach said.

"Zach, did you know I was a sheriff before I retired?" Alen asked.

"No, I didn't. Do you think you can help me find who did this? I'm not sure how hard they will work to solve the murder of a foreign national. And all of Kaylee's friends and employees are English speaking. Maybe you can find out more than the Italian-speaking police," Zach reasoned.

"Sure, tell us about Kaylee, her friends, her habits. We'll do whatever we can," Joan said. "Would you prefer some coffee?" she asked, nodding to his untouched water glass.

"Yes, I'll even make it. I need something to do. I haven't slept. It makes me feel better that we can do something besides sit and wait," he said walking to the kitchen. Joan and Alen silently followed him, waiting for him to share any information.

"Kaylee never really fit in here. She had no desire to learn Italian, but she also didn't like the heavy Italian accent when the Venetians spoke English. That's one of the reasons she started her company, My Venice My Way. They specialize in tour guides from the United States and Great Britain who are native English speakers. She has eight employees and runs multiple tours a day, seven days a week.

My wife, Lesley, does the books and payroll for her. She can get you the employees' names and phone numbers. She didn't have an office. Her best friend since she got here is Zoe. Zoe works for the tour company. She doesn't have a boyfriend unless one popped up in the last week. She and I had lunch together on Tuesdays. I can't believe she's gone. I can't believe someone would harm her. She was sweet and nice. And so pretty. Why would anyone do this to her?" he asked Alen.

"I don't know. But we'll try to find out. So, you can't think of anyone she didn't get along with or any problems she was having?" Alen answered.

They were sitting around the kitchen table, drinking coffee, and Joan had gotten a pad and pen to make notes. For now, she was happy to let Alen ask the questions. She had not had to deal directly with a loved one before and was afraid she might seem insensitive. She shouldn't have worried. Twenty-five years of answering 911 emergency calls meant she was well trained to talk to people and keep them calm in a crisis. But investigations were still new to her.

"I can't think of anyone in the city that would wish her harm. The killer almost has to be a tourist. And that means it's going to be harder to find and catch them. They may have already left the city," he said frantically.

"I think talking to the employees of My Venice My Way will be the best place to start. Did Kaylee conduct any of the tours, or did she just manage the others?" Joan asked now.

"She would do a tour if she couldn't fill a spot at the last-minute kind of thing. Lesley can tell you more about the operation. Do you want me to see if she can bring the girls and come into the city?" Zach asked.

"No, we don't need her to do that. I can get the information I need from her on the phone. I'm betting she was up with you all night too," Joan said.

## Victimized in Venice

"Yeah, she was. I guess we all need some sleep. But I can't sleep right now," Zach said. "And I'm waiting for Ray to call back to see what's going to happen now after he talks to Pamela. I'm not even sure why he's involving her. I understand she's Kaylee's mother. But when things got tough with Kaylee, she called Ray and said she couldn't deal with Kaylee anymore and he had ten days to get her to Italy. Getting her here that quickly was problematic. The girl didn't even have a passport, and expediting all the necessary paperwork was expensive. The whole thing hurt Kaylee a lot. Lately, Pamela started communicating with Kaylee more often and seemed to be trying to mend the relationship. I wish I knew what Kaylee would want. I guess I do know. She's lived here for four years, but I don't think she ever felt like Venice or Italy was home. Not like Holly and Ray and Lesley and I do," Zach rambled.

"Would you like to lie down in the guest room while you wait for Ray to call?" Joan asked. As she did, she remembered the picture on the nightstand and wondered if seeing the photo would help or make him feel worse.

"Maybe I could try that. I feel wasted and useless right now," Zach answered.

"Give me just a minute to freshen the room. Give Alen Lesley's phone number. I'll call her while you're resting." Joan said. She hustled off to hide the photo of Kaylee. She didn't want the photo to upset Zach and thought it was best not to take a chance, she reasoned.

When she returned to the kitchen, she addressed her husband.

"I have one question, and then I think you need to leave for your cooking class. Should we try to meet with the employees all at once or individually? Which would be best?"

"Individually. That way we can compare their stories. I don't have to go to this class," he said.

"Oh, yes, you do! I like eating your cooking. I'll call Lesley and get the info. You'll only be gone a few hours. I'll stay here with Zach," she said.

"Promise you won't start without me?" he asked.

"You've turned around from not wanting to investigate crimes," she said in answer.

"Now, it's more personal for some reason. Even though I never met her, finding who did this feels personal. And you were heavy and sad yesterday. Today you seem more energetic," he answered.

"Yeah, I've moved past sad to mad, I guess. What if the killer is a tourist? Someone who's already gone? How will we ever find them?" she wondered aloud.

"Usually, someone somewhere knows something or saw something, even if they didn't realize it at the time. Also, hopefully, they maintain a list of clients or customers. If they accept credit cards, that will provide names of clients."

"Yeah, a lot of these tour companies work on a pay what you want structure. You tip the tour guide at the end in cash what you want to pay. I have to give a name and email address at least when I've booked even free tours online. Maybe Lesley has access to all that too. I'll find out. Now run along, don't be late," she said. Once he was out the door, she called Lesley to get all the information she could.

~***~

"Hello?"

"Lesley, it's Joan Arny, I'm ---"

"Hi, Joan. I guess Zach made it to you guys to tell you what happened. I don't know what to do. I don't know how to handle this."

"Well, first, take a deep breath. I'm happy to help any way I can. We can all work together to get through this."

"Oh? Helping families through a crisis is part of the house-sitting process? How bizarre," Lesley answered.

"Before we retired, Alen was a sheriff, and for twenty-five years, I was a 911 dispatch operator. So, yeah, we are familiar with getting families through all kinds of crises. And you wouldn't believe how many situations we've encountered since we started house sitting. Let's start with what's the most pressing problem on your mind?"

"I feel like a soulless witch at the minute. Ray and Holly are trying to figure out what to do with the body, Zach wants to catch who did it, and I'm sitting here wondering what to do with the business. Which is likely the least important thing, but that's what I'm wondering. What do I do? Do I shut the tours down or keep them going? Eight people are counting on paychecks this week. How do I tell them all that she's gone? They are going to ask about their jobs. I would. But what do I tell them? If I say, I don't know, they'll all be looking for new jobs, and by the end of the week, we might not have a choice with no employees. We never talked about survivorship. I know better. I was an accountant and a business advisor before we came here. But she was only twenty years old. Can you tell me what to do?"

Lesley was panicking. And Joan suddenly realized that Lesley's dilemma could also be her own. If the employees scattered in the wind, it would be harder to question them.

"Do you feel like talking about this right now? I might have some suggestions," Joan asked.

"Yes. Thank you. I don't have anyone else to talk to. Zach, Ray, and Holly are grieving Kaylee's loss, and it doesn't feel right to ask about the business end. But this is a seven-day-a-week business and we have bookings for weeks in advance. I need to figure out what to do," Lesley said. Her voice still stressed but not as frantic as before.

"Why don't you start by explaining the business to me. How does the company work, and who does what?"

"We offer tours during four separate time slots a day for scheduled tours. Each tour is two hours long. For each slot, there are two simultaneous tours. The times are 9 to 11, and 11 to 1, 1 to 3 and 3 to 5. For each time we offer one American tour and one British tour. We have four guides working each day and we have eight employees in total. It's not an easy job, sometimes dealing with tourists can be stressful. And dealing with the crowds too. But if for some reason they missed a shift, because of illness or whatever, that employee lost a shift for that pay period. She didn't allow them to swap shifts either. She called it a fine balance. So, if someone missed work, she filled that slot."

"Okay, I understand. Are all the tours the same?" Joan asked.

"No. That's another thing she did. Each of the four dailies is different. She figured out that if she worked the tour schedule that way and a tourist was in town for just one day, she could theoretically take all their tour dollars. Each of the guides is trained to give the four available tours."

"She sounds like a very bright businesswoman. And I assume the two tours offered at the same time were one in U.S. English and one in British English to the same places?"

"And you would be wrong. There are so many tours going on at the same time in the city. The tours with a U.S. guide were offered in the afternoon with the U.K. guide and also reversed. Like this. 9 a.m. U.S. would be 3 p.m. U.K.. My Venice My Way guides would never be in the same place at the same time." Lesley explained.

"Amazing. She must have been a math whiz in school. So, she did the business side of things and the guides did the tours?" Joan said.

"You would think. And she did do well in school. But when it came to money, taxes, income, payroll, you would have thought she'd never seen a number before in her life," Lesley said.

"She went out there," Lesley continued, "contacted all the cruise companies and convinced them to put her brochures in all the staterooms. She was the face of the business. But I handle all the real numbers."

"Is the business doing well, then?" Joan asked.

"Shockingly, yes. There are four types of tour companies here. The first one is the legal one. Registered tour guides licensed by the state. They are the only ones legally operating as tour guides. The rest

## Victimized in Venice

sort of fly under the radar. The second is what we call freelance tour guides. They offer free tours with the expectation of a reasonable to hefty tip at the end of the tour. They operate on a cash basis. The third is the self-guided tour app. They aren't located here and operate as a phone app from another country. Therefore, they aren't governed by Italian law. And then, there's My Venice My Way. Kaylee rolled the freelance and app tours into one model. We operate as a foreign entity operating in Italy. Because we only offer tours in English, instead of being considered a tour company, we are an English service company. Instead of offering free tours to evade government regulations and taxes like the other freelancers, she charges a premium price for the luxury of the tour being in your native language. Her advertising promotes tours you can understand, in your native language with no accents," Lesley explained.

"Hmm, all this makes me wonder why Ray and Holly weren't as proud of her as they were of Zach. At only twenty years old, she came up with a brilliant business model, it sounds like," Joan said.

"Yep, and here we are, back to where we started. What do we do with the company now? Venice is a small town. Once word gets out that she's gone, the news will spread through Venice faster than the Great Fire of London," Lesley said.

"I assume, at her age, she probably didn't have a will. But it sounds like you knew her business personality as well as anyone. What do you think she would want? If the business was to be transferred to someone, who would she want the company to go to?" Joan asked. But the answer came from behind her instead of through the phone which she had on speaker so she could take notes while they talked.

"Lesley," Zach said strongly, startling Joan. He put a hand on her shoulder. "I'm sorry, I didn't mean to scare you."

"Zach?" Lesley said through the phone line.

"Yeah, Babe. I was resting here after telling Alen and Joan what was going on and waiting for Ray to call back. But you're the only logical one to take over the company. If you want to, that is. Holly and

Ray couldn't care less about it. I don't have the time or desire. The only problem would be the girls if you needed to take a shift because someone was out. But, with the money the company is making, we could hire a nanny to help out with the girls, if you wanted."

"I am a long way away from wanting to think about a nanny. But I don't have any problem taking on more of the responsibilities with the company. Maybe one or two of the guides would be interested in extra money more than time off and be willing to fill in when needed. Or maybe we could hire more guides. I don't know. But how do I tell them all that Kaylee is gone and reassure them that they still have jobs?"

Joan was thinking. "I agree that you sound like the perfect person to take the business over. That is, if you want to. Let me think for a minute," Joan said.

"Have you heard back from Ray?" Lesley asked Zach.

"Yeah. They've decided to have her sent back to the U.S." he answered.

"So, they aren't coming back early?" Lesley asked.

"No, they are going to wait for her. The police said they could release the body in as few as ten days or as long as thirty. He's contacting the Embassy to see if they can speed things up. They did tell him the time of death was between 8 p.m. and midnight Sunday night. And that the cause of death was strangulation. She was dead before she went into the canal." Zach answered.

"Lesley, how would you feel about me contacting the employees?" Joan asked. "I would like to talk to them to see if they are aware of any tourists Kaylee had a problem with, or anything else. I could start with the four who are off today. Alen will be done with his cooking class before the tours start this afternoon. I would like to experience one before a guide knows who I am, then I could talk to them afterward."

"Yes, thank you so much. The girls are getting restless and I'm exhausted. I can shoot you an email with all their names and phone numbers. You're safe with the two who are working. They aren't allowed to have their phones on. The problem is they all know each other, and once you tell one of them, they'll call the others faster than a Southern Baptist prayer chain,"

"Okay, I think I can prevent that. An old lesson I learned in college," Joan told her.

"This may be confusing, but here goes," Lesley said. "We have four guides from each country. Zoe, Leah, Jenna, and Blake are from the U.S.. "Brandon, Paige, Noah, and Hailey are from the U.K.. Zoe and Hailey are the most important ones to talk to working today, and Zoe is Kaylee's best friend. She has the second or late shift. That means her lunch break is from 1 to 3 p.m. this afternoon. She's dating an Italian; his name is Fabio. I think they usually meet for lunch at a local restaurant. I'll send you the address in the email. The other two guides who are working today are Brandon and Blake. Don't worry about them yet, you can talk to them later. I don't think they'll be much help."

"Okay, and if I understand the system correctly, that means, Hailey will finish her late tour at 3 p.m. right?"

"Right."

"I think what I'll do is start with Zoe. That seems only fair if she's Kaylee's best friend. Then we can talk to Hailey at the end of her tour. How will I find Hailey? Where does her tour end and how can I recognize them?"

"Oh, My Venice My Way's uniform is a red, white, and blue striped Rugby shirt. Think shirts like the gondoliers wear in U.S. and UK colors."

"Okay, send me the rest of the information and we'll get started. I suppose it will be tomorrow before we can take a tour. Send me the work schedule for the rest of the week too. And then try to get some rest. Okay?"

## Chapter Seven

"Zach, why don't you go home? It's not that it isn't nice having you here, but you and Lesley need some rest. And you likely need each other too. You could take turns taking care of the girls. Get something to eat. Take a few days. Have you heard what Ray needs you to do?" Joan asked Zach.

"There isn't much we can do until the police release the body. I know that. Ray is working with the U.S. Embassy. I think they'll help with a lot of the details and red tape of sending her back. There will probably be stuff I need to do later. I really should go to work," he answered.

Recognizing the responsible man for who he was, she realized that he was much like her Alen. Zach realized he had workers counting on him as well as people needing the homes they were working to make inhabitable. But he needed to be reminded of his other responsibilities too. Strong women were often overlooked by their driven men. But even strong women needed their partner from time to time, and this was one of those times.

"I understand you have a lot of people counting on you, Zach. But I bet you are a fair and honest boss, one who works hard, who doesn't ask anyone to do anything you wouldn't do. Am I right?"

"Yes, ma'am. That is how I try to run my business. Thank you for recognizing that in me," he said gratefully.

"And I feel that Lesley is an independent, strong, powerhouse who rarely needs anyone or anything. Is that also accurate?"

"Yes. The woman amazes me with all she does," he replied.

"So, tell me. What would you say to one of your employees who showed up for work the day he discovered a family member died?"

Zach was silent for a moment.

"I would tell him to go home, be with his family. I have his back and work will be waiting for him when he gets back. I understand. It's no different because I'm the boss, right? I'm tired and stressed and on a construction site of any kind, that's a recipe for disaster. Thank you for pointing that out," he said.

"Let me point this out too, your wife is strong. I am too. But when I'm hurting, I don't necessarily need Alen, but I sure want him with me. I bet Lesley would like you to be with her right now too," she said gently and wisely.

"Are you a mom?" Zach asked.

"No. I was never blessed with children. Why?" she asked.

"You would have been a great one. Like mine. I was lying in that room feeling like I was five years old again and sick. I wanted my mom. Thanks for being here. You're a great substitute," he said. He stood up, hugged her, then summoned the elevator.

Joan was able to hold back the tears until he was safely in the elevator and then they flowed like spring rain. To her mind, the comparison was the nicest thing anyone had ever said to her, and she couldn't have asked for a better substitute son.

## Victimized in Venice

She opened the email and printed out Lesley's list of employees using Holly's and Ray's printer while she dried her eyes and sent Alen a text message.

*Meet me at the clock tower at Campo Santa Margherita as soon as you can. Leaving the penthouse now.*

~***~

"Hello, my lovely bride," Alen said as Joan approached him. He was casually leaning against the concrete brick wall of the tower at the end of the plaza. Joan kissed him in greeting.

"Are we having lunch here?" he asked.

"Don't tell me you're starving. I'm betting you've been snacking on delicious cicchetti all morning," she said.

"True. But what about you, my lovely?" he asked.

"No time for that. We have to find Kaylee's best friend, who is supposedly having lunch here with her boyfriend. And we have to break the news to her that her friend is gone before her next tour is scheduled this afternoon," Joan explained to Alen.

"And you think she's going to be a merry tour guide showing off the city after that?" Alen asked.

"Oh, crap! I didn't think of that. I first thought to talk to the guides who were off today, but when Lesley told me that Zoe was Kaylee's best friend, it felt unfair to not tell her first," Joan explained, now distraught and second-guessing her plan.

"Could someone else fill in for her?" Alen asked.

"No. The schedule of how this thing works rivals a complex mathematical theory. If someone couldn't work their shift, Kaylee filled in," Joan told him.

"Well, the way I see it, we have three options. You can call Lesley and see if someone can fill in for her. We talk to her now and no guide shows up for her scheduled tour. Or we wait until the end of her shift. What do you want to do?"

"I spent all morning on the phone with Lesley. She's exhausted, and I sent Zach home to be with her and the girls so they could take shifts trying to get some rest. I don't want to call either of them in case they're sleeping. Now might even be nap time for the girls, and they might all be sleeping. So that isn't an option. These tours are paid for in advance, so there would be some angry tourists if a guide doesn't show up. I have all the employee's names and phone numbers, and I know who is off today, so I could call around and see if someone could cover the tour. But none of them have ever heard of me, and that would just lead to a whole lot of questions I don't want to answer. I suppose the only acceptable answer is to wait until after her shift. I was planning to talk to Hailey, the British guide on duty at the end of her shift at 3 p.m. The tour ends at Palazzo Ariani Minotto Cicogna, not too far from here," she told him.

"Have you eaten today?" Alen asked her.

"No," she answered sheepishly. "And now that you mention it, I am a little hungry. I guess with the excitement of trying to find out who would harm Kaylee, I completely forgot about eating," she admitted.

"Let's get you something to eat, you can catch me up on what you learned, and we'll still make it in plenty of time to catch the end of Hailey's tour," he suggested.

"Have I mentioned that I love how reasonable you are?" she asked as he took her hand and steered her toward a restaurant called the Orange Bar.

"Nope. You haven't mentioned it all. At least not today," he teased while he held a chair for her to sit on under an umbrella in a lovely garden inside the restaurant's interior courtyard. The outside dining area was surrounded on three sides by palaces and made for a romantic lunch for two. Alen wasn't hungry following the samplings from his cooking class, but Joan enjoyed a good American-style hamburger, and then they were on their way to meet up with Hailey after she finished her last tour of the day.

~***~

## Victimized in Venice

Alen and Joan tried to assume the posture of innocent tourists in front of the Palazzo Ariani Minotto Cicogna. They listened to Hailey in her British English accent explain that the palace was built as a family home for the Ariani family in the thirteenth century. In the seventeenth century, with no more surviving heirs, the palace transferred to the Pasqualigo family. After transferring several times, a nun converted the palace from a home to a college. The palace has been owned by the province since 1870 and now houses a technical institute. That concluded Hailey's tour. She shook hands with her eight apparent tour customers and when she turned to go, Joan called out to her.

"Hailey?"

The young lady turned and looked at Joan as if she was trying to place her.

"You don't know me. My name is Joan Arny, and this is my husband, Alen. We are friends of the Roberts family, and I wondered if we might speak with you. It's really important. Could we buy you a coffee, a drink, something?" Joan asked.

"Um, thank you for the offer. But I have to be going. I have an appointment," Hailey said looking not unlike a scared animal.

"Yeah, I would be leery of a stranger approaching me too," Alen said. "Hailey, Lesley Wise sent us to talk to you. Something has happened to Kaylee. We must speak with you. We can talk in a public place where you feel safe. If you want to call a friend to be with you, that's fine too. We can wait. Or you can call Lesley and verify that she sent us to talk with you."

"Kaylee? What happened? Is she sick? Hurt? Should we go to the hospital?"

"How about we find a place to sit down. You choose where. Someplace you are comfortable," Joan said gently.

"Okay. Both of the restaurants near here are already closed for the afternoon. But I think the Blu Bar should be open. We have to cross the bridge and walk a few blocks if that's okay," Hailey explained.

"Sure, that's fine," Joan said. She and Alen followed the lady in the red, white, and blue, striped shirt to the bar.

"So, how do you know Kaylee?" Hailey asked. Joan noticed that she still seemed suspicious, and Joan didn't blame her. She would be too.

"We haven't met Kaylee," Joan answered. We know her parents, and of course, Zach and Lesley."

"You mean her dad and stepmum, right? Ray and..." she stopped. She realized she might be walking into a trap and stopped sharing information. "Her real mom doesn't live here," Hailey said.

"Yes, right. We are house-sitting for Ray and Holly while they are in the United States. We're professional house sitters, retired from the U.S. Alen was a sheriff there and I worked as a dispatcher for the emergency dispatch center," Joan explained, still working to put the girl at ease.

They reached the bar and Hailey entered first, selecting a table next to a window. "We need to order at the bar. What would you like? I can order it," Hailey said.

"How about I order for us, it's our treat. What would you like, Hailey?" Alen said. The girl thought for a minute and then answered.

"Just a coffee, please. Black," she said. Alen looked at Joan, who nodded and he went to the bar.

"When was the last time you saw Kaylee?" Joan asked.

"She was at a birthday party Sunday night with Zoe and me. Why what happened?"

"What time was the party and where?" Joan asked.

"At The Irish Pub. The party started at eight. We closed the place down at two. But Kaylee left early. I'm not sure when, but she was already gone when Zoe and I left. Please tell me what's going on. I'm starting to freak out here," Hailey said.

"I'm so sorry to have to tell you this, and there is no easy way to say it. But Kaylee died," Joan said.

"What? That can't be right. She's too young! She's healthy. Why are you saying this to me? I have to go," Hailey said and started to stand up. Alen was there, holding a tray with three cups of coffee and she nearly bumped into him.

"Hailey, please stay. We need your help to figure out what happened to Kaylee," Alen said softly. She sat back down.

"What happened? When did she die? How?" Hailey asked. Joan took a deep breath.

"She was murdered," Joan said.

"What? Murders don't happen in Venice! When?"

"Sunday night. The police estimate she died between eight p.m. and midnight. But you saw her during that time. You may be able to help us narrow down the time, and that might help us catch her killer," Alen said.

"Well, it was a party, I wasn't exactly watching the clock. There were a lot of people crammed in the place. I got to the party at about 8:15, I think. Zoe and Kaylee were already there. But after that, I'm not sure. I didn't realize who came and went and when would be important. As I said, Kaylee was gone when we left. Maybe she left early and walked home? She and Zoe are best friends. She probably told Zoe when she was leaving, but she didn't tell me. Hopefully, Zoe can tell you more," Hailey said.

"Hailey, I understand this is hard. If you can think of anyone who would want to harm Kaylee, the information would be helpful. Maybe someone she had a fight with or a disagreement?" Joan asked.

Hailey thought about it for a few minutes.

"Look, Kaylee is a sweet girl. Sheesh, I mean was. But she doesn't like living in Italy. She doesn't get along well with the locals and she tries to only associate with the other ex-pats from the U.S. and the U.K. But it's not possible to not associate with any locals, you know. There is this one waitress at a restaurant we like to go to. It's inexpensive and owned by a Brit. But this waitress is Venetian. She and Kaylee were always butting heads. The waitress is trying to learn

English, and Kaylee was always correcting her pronunciation. She wasn't always nice about correcting her either. But that's the only person I can think of," Hailey explained.

"Do you know the waitress's name? And what's the name of the restaurant?" Joan asked.

"Her name is Gisella. The restaurant is called London Chips. It's on Calle Lunga near the Ponte degil Scalzi bridge. It's close to Kaylee's apartment, my apartment and also Noah and Brandon's apartment. We used to meet there a lot. Have you told them yet?" Hailey asked.

"No, you're the first one we've told. We're planning to tell Zoe when her tour ends, then we will talk to the others. The best situation is if we talk to them before anyone tells them what happened. It's easier to think about situations and circumstances that could lead to violence before the shock hits of knowing a victim. It might even take a few days for us to get to everyone," Joan said.

"Well, that's not going to happen," Hailey said. "This is a small town and news travels fast. Even if Zoe and I can manage to not tell anyone. But Kaylee was our friend. Not just our boss. Even if I only told my parents, they are friends with Jenna's parents. See where I'm going? I would like to go with you to tell Zoe. I honestly almost didn't, shouldn't have come with you. If my parents knew I walked off with a couple of strangers, they would kill me."

"I think we need to talk to Zoe," Joan started to say, but Alen interrupted her.

"Thank you for helping us with Zoe," Alen said. "Since they were all together on the night in question, Hailey and Zoe might be able to work together to put the pieces we need into a workable bit of information," he said to Joan.

"We have just enough time to get to the end of Zoe's tour before she finishes if we leave now," Hailey said, standing.

Joan and Alen followed as she led the way.

# Chapter Eight

"Where will Zoe's tour end?" Joan asked Hailey.

"Doge's Palace. It's near San Marco Plaza," she explained.

"We're familiar with it," Alen said, remembering the coffee that cost them fifteen euros each in the square.

"They walked up to the palace where they spotted the now-familiar red, white, and blue, shirt on a young lady. Alen and Joan knew they had found Zoe, supposedly Kaylee's best friend since she arrived in Italy at the age of sixteen.

When the tour was over, Zoe walked toward her friend, Hailey.

"What are you doing here? In your work shirt, no less. You know the rules. Kaylee is adamant about no two of us being seen together in our work shirts, and she'll kill you if she finds out," Zoe said to Hailey, not even realizing Joan and Alen were standing with her.

"I don't think that's going to happen," Hailey said, sadly. "Zoe, this is Joan. And I'm sorry, sir, what was your name?"

"Alen," he answered.

"Yeah, Joan and Alen. They are house-sitting for Kaylee's dad and stepmom. They need to talk to you," Hailey said. At that moment she decided she couldn't be the one to tell Zoe because she still couldn't say the words. Maybe keeping this all a secret wouldn't be as hard as she first thought.

"What about?" Zoe asked Hailey.

"Something happened to Kaylee. We all need to talk, but let's go somewhere we can sit down," Hailey suggested.

"Let's take the ferry across to Giudecca. There's an inexpensive café, not like these overpriced ones," Zoe suggested. "And maybe Kaylee won't bump into us together in our work shirts. Come on, the ferry is this way," she said and they all followed her.

Once they were on the ferry that would take them straight across the canal to the next island, Joan asked her burning question.

"Why are you not supposed to be together in your work shirts?" Joan asked.

Zoe looked at Hailey as if to silently ask, who are these people? And should we be talking to them? Hailey nodded her head at Zoe.

"In Venice, tour guides are supposed to be licensed. We aren't. We have to have distinctive shirts so that the people who pay for our tours can find us, but Kaylee doesn't want us in the same area at the same time because then they look like work shirts and will call attention to us," Zoe explained.

"Okay, now I understand," Joan said.

The *traghetto*, or ferry, pulled into its dock and they disembarked, with Zoe leading the way to a coffee shop facing the water.

Once again, Alen asked what everyone wanted and went to place the order. The three ladies sat at a table for four.

"So, spill," Zoe said. "What's Kaylee done now? I can't believe her dad is sending the house-sitter out after her like a babysitter or something."

"It's not like that," Hailey said, and then waited for Joan to tell her what was going on.

"Zoe, Hailey told us that you and Kaylee were at a birthday party Sunday night at the Irish Pub. Do you remember what time Kaylee left?"

"No. I don't. Why? Did she miss Daddy's curfew?" Zoe asked sarcastically. "Is spying on his daughter part of your duties as the house-sitter?"

"I'm not here because of her father," Joan said patiently. "I'm here because something horrible happened to Kaylee after she left the party. And I'm trying to find answers. My husband was a sheriff, and we're just trying to help out the family right now," she explained.

"Oh, what happened to her? Was she mugged?" as thoughts were going through Zoe's head before Joan could answer, "Crap, she wasn't raped, was she? Flaming cruise ship tourists, she shouldn't have left alone," Zoe said.

"No, Zoe. She died," Joan said.

"What? She didn't seem drunk; did she stumble into the canal? What the heck happened?" Zoe asked.

"She was murdered," Joan said and then waited for Zoe to process the news.

"What? What is she talking about?" Zoe asked Hailey.

"I know, I can't wrap my mind around her being gone either. But according to Joan, we might have been the last ones to see her," Hailey said and began to cry.

"Crap, I shouldn't have let her go home alone," Zoe said.

"She told you she was going home?" Joan asked Zoe.

"Yeah, she wasn't feeling well, she said. She said she wanted to go home. I told her I would go with her. But she said she didn't want me to miss the party and that if I came back to the party by myself, that was no different than her going home alone. I walked out with her to the taxi stand, and then I returned to the party. It's probably a twenty-minute walk for her from there to home, but since she wasn't feeling well, I told her she should take a taxi," Zoe told them as Alen served their drinks from a tray. Zoe and Hailey had both opted for a spritz while he and Joan enjoyed another coffee. He was relieved that this café was reasonably priced.

"Do you remember what time that was?" Joan asked.

Alen watched both girls carefully for any sign of silent communication. Hailey sat with her head down, silently crying. She wasn't communicating with Zoe at all that he could see. He also noticed that Zoe's phone sat face down on the table. He was confident no text messages were coming in for her to see either. He felt comfortable that they were getting accurate statements from Zoe.

"I don't know. I wasn't paying attention to the time. I think it was pretty early though. If I had to guess I would say around eight. It didn't feel like we had been there long. What happened to her? Where?"

"We aren't sure where the crime happened. She was strangled. And then she was dropped into the canal, where she was found the next morning," Joan said, intentionally leaving out the details about the duffel bag and that she and Alen were the ones who found her. That fact seemed like a coincidence of divine intervention proportion. Alen sought her hand under the table and squeezed it. He approved of her omissions.

"That's just awful! I can't believe this happened to one of us," Zoe said. It appeared the news was starting to sink in.

"Zoe, can you think of anyone who would want to hurt Kaylee?" Joan asked.

"No. Why would anyone ever kill someone?"

"Usually, jealousy, greed, love, money, passion," Alen said.

"Well, Kaylee didn't date. I'm not sure why. She's beautiful. All the Italian men flirted with her. She never gave them the time of day. Never flirted back. She had no more money than any of the rest of us. She was smart. She started a great business. Yeah, some of the local tour guides might have had a grudge against her, but not enough to kill for. She didn't socialize with the locals. And actually, she didn't like dealing with them either. We have a fairly tight small circle of friends," Zoe answered.

"Whose birthday were you celebrating on Sunday?" Joan asked.

"Amber Townsend. We don't know her all that well. She's not part of our circle of friends. She just moved here from the U.S. and is a few years older than us. My brother's best friend is trying to date her, and he threw this big surprise party for her. We hadn't even met her…we just went because usually, Sunday nights are pretty dead in Venice."

"I see. Okay. Can you think of anyone that Kaylee has had issues with lately?"

"As I said, she didn't like having to work with the locals. She was complaining a lot about the maintenance guy her landlord hired. And there is this one waitress. They were always needling each other," Zoe said.

"Gisella at London Chips?" Joan asked.

"Yeah, that's her. Are the police investigating her? Honestly, I can see how she might feel Kaylee was bullying her. But Venetians aren't all up in arms about bullying like people are in the states. They just deal with it here. At least I thought they did," Zoe said.

"We aren't aware of what the police are doing right now. Hailey told us about Gisella. We'll look into it. If you think of anyone else, please call us. Here are our phone numbers," Alen said.

"Can you two ladies not tell anyone about this? We would like to talk to all the employees one on one. At least through tomorrow?" Joan asked Zoe and Hailey.

"Yeah," Zoe said. "I don't want to be the one to have to tell them. Hailey, do you want to stay at my place tonight?"

"Uh-huh, you and I can talk without having to tell anyone else. Maybe we can think of someone else. Of course, with all the tourists in town, it might have been random, right? Maybe the killer isn't anyone we know? Because, that's really freaking me out," Hailey said.

"It could be random, and that certainly does happen. But it's very rare," Alen told them honestly.

"Are you both okay?" Joan asked.

They both nodded their heads that they were.

"Can we get together tomorrow night with whoever else you've talked to," Zoe asked.

"Sure. If you want to set a place to meet up, we can tell people you'll be getting together," Joan said.

"Just tell them to come to my apartment. Everyone knows where I live. Anytime after five is good. I'm off tomorrow," Zoe said.

"Zoe, I have one more question. And as her best friend, you can probably answer it better than anyone," Joan said.

"Okay, what is it?"

"You and Hailey both expressed that Kaylee didn't love Venice. That she didn't like the locals. I'm aware that her mother sent her here when she was sixteen. But she's twenty now. If she hated Venice and Italy so much, why didn't she go back to the United States?"

"Economics," Zoe said.

"But we understand it's very expensive to live here," Alen said.

"It is. But Kaylee had it made. Her folks aren't aware of how well her business is doing. Except Lesley does because she does the books. But Kaylee was smart when it came to business. She had Lesley sign a nondisclosure agreement. She can't even tell Zach what's happening with the business. Her father thought she was barely getting by, so he paid her rent for her. Not many young people can afford to live here on the wages you can earn here and especially without roommates. Noah and Brandon are roommates, and Jenna still lives at home with her parents. The rest of us have some form of help from our families to not have roommates. Most locals don't have that option. But actually, we all make pretty good money, especially Kaylee," Zoe explained.

"And that was enough to keep her here?" Joan said.

"Well, that, plus, if she went back, she would need a car, a job, housing. Being homeschooled over the internet here basically means in the U.S. people feel we have the equivalent of a GED. Jobs paying the equivalent of what we make here aren't an option for those of us who chose not to go to college," she told them. "Oh, and if you guys want to come tomorrow night too, you're welcome. I'm sure we all want to know what happened to our friend," Zoe said.

"Thank you for the invitation. We'll see how things go. I'm sure we'll talk to you soon. We are very sorry for your loss," Joan said as she hugged each one of the young ladies goodbye.

When they returned to the penthouse, Alen took Carina for her evening walk and agreed to bring home a pizza while Joan called Lesley to see who was working the next day and where.

Over pizza, she told Alen what she learned from Lesley.

"According to Lesley, she did have a nondisclosure agreement. But she says as a former accountant, she was accustomed to not talking about client finances. She figured that since Kaylee is gone, she could talk to me about it. Especially if she is going to take over the business. Kaylee was making a lot of money," Joan told him.

"Did she say how much?" Alen asked.

"She told me that she's feeling uncomfortable and guilty. Earlier today she was worried about what she should do with the business. Now the thought of the business being hers has her pretty excited. According to Lesley, each of the tour guides makes $1,600 U.S. every two weeks. Kaylee paid Lesley $1,300 for taking care of the finances. With no overhead, no expenses, Kaylee's profit turned out to be over $11,000 every two weeks," Joan said.

"Holy anchovies! We're in the wrong business, Joan," he exclaimed.

"My thoughts too," she said.

"I don't blame Lesley for being excited about that kind of money. Anyone would be. But wait. Lesley is the only person who knows how much money Kaylee was making, right?"

"It looks and sounds that way. Why?"

"It would be a motive for murder. That's why," Alen said.

"No. No way. The reason she's so excited is that she wants to funnel that money into Zach's housing projects, not for herself," Joan defended.

"It's still a motive for murder," he repeated.

# Chapter Nine

A<small>LEN AND</small> J<small>OAN HAD AGREED</small> to disagree about the likelihood of Lesley being a suspect. During Carina's morning walk, they decided how they wanted to handle the day. They would divide and conquer. Not themselves. Well, maybe themselves too. Noah and Paige were conducting the day's British English tours, and Leah and Jenna were conducting the U.S. English tours. If they each took two of the day's guides, that would only leave two employees left for them to interview.

"I realize this might seem silly, but something is telling me to take one of these tours to see how it goes," Joan told him as they were walking in Parco Savorgnan with Carina.

"I admit, I had the same thought. Always trust your gut in a situation like this," Alen said.

"If we both take the first tour of the day, that guide will be taking their two-hour break at the end of the tour. We could talk to them while the second tour of the day was happening and catch those two when they finish. By three o'clock we could have talked to all four of them. We would still have time to try to meet up with the other two. What do you think?"

"I think you're planning for one of us to take a U.S. tour and talk to the U.S. people, and the other will take the U.K. tours. Right? So, you're trying to get away from me for the day?" Alen pouted.

"Oh, Honey, that's not true. And I also believe that although you appear to be pouting, it's all an act," she told him.

"That's the problem with being with the same woman for close to two decades," he complained as he grasped her hand and laid a gentle kiss upon it.

"Are you bored with me already?" she asked playfully.

"No, somehow you still manage to surprise me daily. But you seem to know everything about me," he said.

"That's the law of marriage. We, that is women, have to constantly evolve to remain mysterious to keep you guys interested," she explained.

"And why do we, as men, not have to do that?" he wondered aloud.

"Some do," she teased.

Back at the penthouse, Joan called Lesley to see if there were spaces on the morning tours that she and Alen could join. Lesley gave her the necessary codes so the guide would know they were legitimate participants but refused to charge her. Joan explained their plan for the day. And she asked if she could arrange for Brandon and Blake to meet them, wearing their work shirts, so they could find them at the famous bookstore called Libreria Acqua Alta at 4 p.m. The bookstore was Joan's planned tourist sight for the day, and she reasoned they would get to the bookstore early, browse and then talk to the last two employees there.

As it turned out, both of the morning tours for Alen and Joan covered sights they experienced on their self-guided tour. But they weren't going to see the sights, Joan reminded Alen when he groaned. She promised he would enjoy the meetup place this afternoon, and

## Victimized in Venice

told him as soon as he finished talking with his second guide for the day, to go to the bookstore where she would meet up with him.

"Do you want to take the Americans or the Brits?" Joan offered.

"I'll take the Brits. At least listening to the accent might make the tour more interesting," he said, smiling mischievously at her.

"Alen, I swear. In almost eighteen years together I haven't heard you complain as much as you have about these tours. What's up? Are you not enjoying them?" She asked concerned.

"No, Sweetheart. I'm just playing. Venice is beautiful. It is, and once I learn more about the stories of its history, I'm sure I'll fall in love with the city as much as you are. It's just at first, I was complaining about not wanting to solve mysteries, and now I'm okay with solving them because I like solving them with you. So, I have to complain about something else. I wouldn't want you to get bored with me. The tour would be much more interesting if we were doing it together, that's all," he said.

"Why would it be more fun?" she asked confused.

"Because I would be holding your hand, and when I got bored with the Venice views, I could look at you," he said sweetly.

"That's almost funny. Some days I feel as old as some of these buildings," she mumbled.

"You're a goddess that never ages," he said.

"Oh, brother. Just think how much more you'll appreciate me after a few hours away from me. Seriously, though. So many people worry about all the hours together after they retire. I'm thankful that we still enjoy each other enough that a few hours apart don't feel like a retreat, a vacation. Okay, you have, Noah this morning and Paige afterward. The morning tour runs nine to eleven. The second tour is eleven to one. Noah will be on break during Paige's tour, then Paige will go on break at one. After you talk to her, meet up with me at the bookstore. Lesley is going to have the remaining employees, Brandon and Blake meet us at the bookstore at four. Until they arrive, we can explore the famous bookstore," she told him.

"A bookstore? *That's* the super fun and interesting place you were planning for us to explore today?" he asked.

"Yep, that was it. It's different and quirky and a great photo op for me. Here are the addresses to find your guides and the bookstore address," she said, handing him a piece of paper. "Just remember to leave yourself time after talking to Noah, to get to Paige at the end of her tour. I don't know where she would go for her break, okay?" she reminded him.

"Got it, Captain. Who are you talking with today, and where will you be?" he asked. He was writing something on a piece of paper.

"Jenna and Leah. The schedule looks like all the churches. Maybe I'll get some divine inspiration," she said.

Alen handed Joan a piece of paper, mimicking her. The note said, *Text me at 2 p.m. Let's have lunch*. It was signed at the bottom with a heart and inside the heart, he had written JA+AA. Joan giggled.

"You've got it, handsome. I do like what Venice is doing for you. It's making you even more romantic than usual," she said and kissed him as they entered the elevator to start their day of interviews.

~***~

After the tour, Joan approached Jenna.

"Jenna, thank you for a lovely tour. Zach and Lesley Wise sent me. I was wondering if I could talk to you, maybe buy you a coffee or lunch?" she said.

"They sent someone to check on me? Gah! I know my tours. I perform them flawlessly. I might miss one unimportant word, but it's not a big deal. Why are they checking on me? Did someone report something?" Jenna responded.

## Victimized in Venice

"No, no, it's nothing like that. I need to talk to you about Kaylee. Something happened to her. I agree, your tour was flawless," Joan explained.

"Oh. I'm sorry. Everyone says I need to work on my self-esteem and my perfectionism problem. I'm sorry I got so defensive. What's wrong with Kaylee?"

"How about we find a comfortable place to talk? Do you know someplace near here?"

"Yeah, sure. I go to a café around the corner. That's where I usually take my break. I read. It relaxes me before the next tour," she said. While they walked, Joan tried to steer the conversation away from Kaylee. She was interested in her newest discovery.

"From your comment I assume all the My Venice My Way tours are standardized. There's a script you all memorize?"

"Yes, ma'am. Kaylee wrote them. And she's a stickler for memorizing them perfectly. Even the little words like *an, the, and,* must be in their proper places. We have to pass an oral and written test on them before we can work a specific route. But you know, sometimes, when you do the same thing over and over, your mind wanders and something might not come out exactly right. It still means the same thing. I've heard of other tour companies using shoppers to check up on their guides. I assumed that's what you were when you said Lesley and Zach sent you. Though Zach doesn't usually have anything to do with the tour business. Here's the café," she said, leading Joan inside a small café.

They approached the counter together. Jenna ordered a chamomile tea, and Joan ordered a coffee.

"Would you like something to eat?" Joan asked Jenna. "I assume this is your lunch break."

"No, I don't eat when I'm working. I get nervous and it doesn't end well," Jenna said.

"Sounds like you're like me and a bit of an introvert," Joan sympathized.

"That would be an understatement. My parents tease me that I love Carnival because it means Lent is coming. And that I give up people for Lent. I wish I could give up people all the time," Jenna said. "You said something happened to Kaylee. What's going on? Did someone finally bust her knee caps or something?" Jenna asked.

"Wow, that's an unusual question," Joan said, surprised.

"Yeah. Sorry. Sometimes my imagination runs away from me. The result of reading too many books, I guess," Jenna answered.

"Well, what do you think is a reason someone would want to cause harm to Kaylee? It sounds like you don't like her much," Joan asked.

"I don't like her. It's not a secret. She's a mean girl, in my opinion. When you said something happened to her, my first thought was someone fought back," Jenna said.

"That raises a couple of questions. First, if you don't like her, why do you work for her? And secondly can you think of anyone in particular, that might cause her harm?" Joan asked, hoping two questions at once weren't too much, but she couldn't wait for the answers.

"Zach got me the job with the tour company. I'm one of the biggest anomalies in Venice. I'm a poor American. I still live with my parents, and the apartment we were renting was being converted to a tourist rental. They raised the rent so high we couldn't afford to stay. Even with both my parents, my brother, and I working. My family owns a business cleaning rental property for absentee owners. There are about 7,000 rentals offered on the internet for tourists, but most of the property owners don't even live here. They need the spaces cleaned when people check out, but they don't want to pay much. I still do that when I'm not working here. Anyway, Zach helped us find an apartment we could afford and got me hired on here. I make as much in two weeks doing this as two of us make in a month cleaning," she explained.

"Okay, I understand. How did you come to live in Venice?" she asked simply out of curiosity.

"An age-old story. We were doing just fine in the U.S. My parents were divorced. My mom met and fell in love with Antonio, who was visiting a cousin in the U.S. But he couldn't get a green card in the states. So, she picked us all up and moved us here. For love. What a romantic story, huh? Except for the poor kids who now have to work twelve hours a day to help pay the living expenses," Jenna said.

"I'm so sorry, Jenna. Does your brother also work for the tour company?"

"No, he's only fourteen, so he's too young. It's okay. I'm sorry. I shouldn't be venting. Anyway, as for Kaylee. Almost anyone who has to deal with her would like to slap her. Or bust a knee cap, or maybe even push her into the canal. She's a prima donna snob who doesn't care how she treats people. She's rude and nasty. So, what happened? Who got to her?"

"That's what we're trying to figure out. Jenna, Kaylee was murdered," Joan said and waited for the response from across the table.

"Oh, crap!" she exclaimed and sat with her mouth open, staring at Joan with wide eyes. She looked surprised and shocked by the news. After a moment she finally found her words.

"Okay, she was a witch, but she didn't deserve to die!"

"When was the last time you saw Kaylee?" Joan asked.

"A few weeks ago, maybe. Payday, I guess. We didn't socialize. Didn't run in the same circles. I imagine this is going to sound insensitive, but I assume I'm out of a job, right?"

"I don't think so. We aren't part of that decision, but I think the family is going to try to keep things running. You need to talk to Lesley about that," Joan told her. "I have to ask you, Jenna. Where were you Sunday night between eight and midnight?"

"At home with my parents. We all work seven days a week, twelve to sixteen hours a day. Whenever we get done cleaning on Sundays, we get in the kitchen and work together to prepare meals for the week," she told Joan.

"It sounds like you have a nice family. I'm sorry your circumstances aren't better. But it's nice that you can all work together toward a common goal," Joan said.

"And now, you're making me feel guilty. Because, yeah, I do love my family. But I've been keeping back some of the money I make working this job toward getting back to the United States. If I lose this job, escaping from here will never happen. I'll be stuck here forever," Jenna said sadly.

"Jenna, how old are you?" Joan asked.

"Twenty-one," she answered.

"I understand you don't feel like it right now. But usually, a lifetime is a really long time. I can tell you from experience that your situation and where you are can change almost overnight. There is no telling where you might be two years, five years, or ten years from now. Less than a year ago, I was going to work at a job I'd been doing for twenty-five years. My life was boring. I didn't even realize it. I thought I was happy. And then something tragic happened, and it changed everything. Now, I'm traveling the world with my husband and meeting new people. My life isn't boring, and I'm wonderfully happy. Change and opportunities will happen for you too. I promise." Joan said.

"Are you saying that Kaylee's tragedy could change my life?" Jenna asked.

"No, that's not exactly what I was thinking, though I suppose this tragedy might be a catalyst for some kind of change. You can make it one if it's important to you. Thank you for talking with me. Here's my phone number, if you think of anyone in particular that might want to hurt Kaylee, please call me. Call Lesley about your job, and Zoe wanted me to tell you that everyone is invited to her

## Victimized in Venice

apartment this evening after work. If you want to go to talk about Kaylee or anything."

"Thanks, I'll be cleaning this afternoon when I finish my tour. The weekend crowd starts arriving tomorrow. Especially with Carnival starting this week. I wish you luck finding out what happened to Kaylee. I'm sorry she died. No one deserves that. And thanks for the tea. If you don't mind, I need to focus on relaxing before my next tour," Jenna said.

"Of course. I hope to see you again under better circumstances. Thanks for the tour, it was very enjoyable. I would have never guessed that you hate doing them. Goodbye, Jenna," Joan said and left the café.

~***~

Meanwhile, Alan was chatting with Noah at a small café where Noah was devouring one of the biggest hamburgers Alen had ever seen. The thought occurred to him as he watched the twenty-something man chomp into his lunch that hamburgers might be the universal food.

"Noah, when was the last time you saw Kaylee?" Alen asked him.

"Mm, I think it was Saturday. Or maybe Friday. No, it was definitely Saturday. I saw her at a costume shop by the Rialto. She was getting fitted for her Carnival costume, I just happened to walk by. I stuck my head in the shop, said hello, and went on my way. Why?" Noah replied.

"Something happened with Kaylee on Sunday. Can you tell me where you were on Sunday evening between eight and midnight?" Alen asked.

"Whoa, you sound like a cop. I can tell you. I was at home with a very sick dog. I had worked all day and came home to a colossal mess and a very upset dog," Noah explained.

"Can anyone verify that?" Alen asked.

"Bloke! Are you serious? Am I under suspicion for something? What did she say? I swear I didn't see Kaylee on Sunday," Noah said.

"No, we're asking everyone, that's all," Alen said. He made a mental note to try and tone down his intensity.

"I worked; I went home. My roommate was away with his girlfriend. So, no, no one can verify I was home. The vet was closed. I called the emergency number, he told me what to do. So, what happened to Kaylee?" Noah asked. "I was planning to go to a party at The Irish Pub Hailey told me about. I went home to change and found a sick dog. I messaged Hailey that I wasn't coming. I suppose all those details conspire to give me the opportunity, right?"

"Kaylee went to that party. But she left early, not feeling well. Someone murdered her," Alen said gently and waited for Noah to process the information.

"Oh, man! Oh, my…, Oh, crap. You can't think I had anything to do with that," Noah said shaking his head back and forth. Alen noticed his hands were shaking also.

"No, Noah. I don't suspect anyone right now. But that is what we are trying to find out. Do you know anyone who would want to hurt Kaylee? Anyone she had a disagreement with or an ongoing problem?"

"Well, yeah, I do. Look, Kaylee was a sweet lady. If you spoke English. If you did things the way she was accustomed to, from America. If you treated her like a princess. They have a phrase here; it translates as there's always time for paying and dying. I always think of karma when I hear it. I don't think that's how they mean it. The only thing I can think of is her latest war was with a guy her landlady hired to do maintenance on Kaylee's apartment. Kaylee was always complaining about something. Her complaints were always stupid little stuff, in my opinion. Caulking was coming loose. A cabinet handle wasn't tight. The closet rod bowed from the weight of her extensive wardrobe. Not serious stuff. I think a slow drip from

## Victimized in Venice

her bathroom faucet was the most serious thing. The landlady got tired of it, so she hired a guy. Part-time, I'm sure, but I think his only job was shutting Kaylee up. She despised him. Didn't think he knew how to do anything right, and she was fairly abusive to him verbally. I was at her apartment one day and heard her tirade on him for myself. The guy didn't speak any English. At least, I don't think he did. I don't think he knew exactly what she was saying, but her tone was unmistakable in any language," Noah said.

"Do you happen to know his name? Or the landlady's name?"

"Um, yeah, let me think about it for a minute. The landlady is a British woman, Sophia Porter. She's pretty well known around town to the British nationals. But the guy's name was Luca, Lupo, no! Lapo. Lapo was his name. I never heard his last name. He lived in the building. I think Sophia gave him a break on rent for dealing with Kaylee. Maybe he decided cheap rent wasn't worth the unpleasant job after all," Noah said.

"Do you have contact information for Sophia Porter? A phone number or email address for her or anything?" Alen asked.

"I never met her exactly, just across the room and gossip type stuff. But from what I've heard, you can find her at Harry's Bar most nights," Noah said.

"Thanks, Noah. You've been very helpful,"

"Thanks for lunch, but I gotta get going to meet my next tour. I'm sorry about Kaylee. I really am. Do you know what's going to happen to the tour company? Like, do I need to be looking for a job?" Noah asked.

"I don't think so. But you should talk to Lesley about that, okay?"

"Yeah, sure. Thanks," Noah said as he stood to leave.

"Oh, Zoe wanted me to tell you that everyone is invited to her apartment after five tonight if you want to go," Alen said.

"Okay, see ya around," Noah said as he left.

SCARLETT MOSS

## Chapter Ten

JOAN NOTICED THAT CARNIVAL COSTUMES were starting to appear. The Carnival costumes in Venice were possibly the most extravagant anywhere. While many countries celebrate Carnival leading up to the Catholic and Christian period of Lent, each country has its unique traditions surrounding the holiday. In Venice, grand balls and galas are accompanied by parades and costume contests. The costumes were so elaborate and expensive, they had to be shown off as much as possible. Most of the costumes were eighteenth-century costumes with wigs, period shoes, and the masks in Venice were often full-face masks where only the eyes showed.

Alen and Joan had gone to New Orleans Mardi Gras years before, and that celebration, while having the similarities, was quite different than here in Venice. Joan was in San Marco Square waiting for Jenna to arrive with her tour. She saw a couple in coordinated outfits in the square acting out a skit. Joan watched, realizing they were speaking in English. When they finished their performance, Joan walked over and introduced herself. She discovered they were from the United States and made the trip to Venice Carnival every year. They had been coming for ten years and each year brought four different costumes to wear throughout the two-week trip. Each year they had one new costume they spent the whole year designing and constructing. Joan caught the red, white, and blue striped shirt out the corner of her eye and excused herself from the interesting couple. She hoped to see them again during their stay.

As Leah thanked her tour clients and they said goodbye to her, she stood off to the side. When the last customer walked away, Joan moved closer to Leah. She was surprised when Leah spoke to her first.

"You must be Joan," Leah said.

"Yes, I am. How did you know?"

"Jenna texted me. She told me it was okay to talk to you," Leah said.

"Oh? As in she permitted you?" Joan asked. She couldn't figure out why the comment struck her in a way that irritated her, but she was instantly annoyed.

"No, nothing like that. Just that you were nice and legit. Not a stranger. Jenna understands I don't like talking to strangers. She just gave me a heads up that I should expect you, and you were safe," Leah said.

"I understand. It's nice to have friends that watch out for you, isn't it? Can I buy you lunch?"

"I won't say no to that. I'm hungry, and since I might not have a job for long, I shouldn't pass up free food, right? But everything right here is crazy-expensive. Let's find someplace more reasonable. Do you mind walking for a bit?"

"Not at all. I'm loving walking in Venice, especially since the Carnival costumes are starting to show up. I can't wait until the city is full of them. I imagine walking through the crowds all dressed in period clothes will feel like traveling back in time," Joan said as they walked.

## Victimized in Venice

"Have you tried the Carnival pastries yet?" Leah asked.

"I don't think so. What are they called?"

"There are three main ones. They are all a variety of deep-fried dough and all amazing. By tomorrow people will be selling them everywhere on the streets as well as in the patisseries. They are locally called *favette,* also called *castagnole, frittole,* and *crostoli* or *galani. Favette* and *frittole* are kind of like flavored doughnut holes. Little fried balls. *Favette* is usually flavored with lemon and anise, *frittole* with raisins and pine nuts, sometimes citrus peel. *Crostoli* and *galani* are the same things, just different shapes. They are both paper-thin doughs flavored with lemon and either grappa or rum. I like grappa ones better. Crostoli are cut into triangles, and galani is like a twisted ribbon," Leah said.

Joan recognized that she must be one of those people who were chatty when they were nervous.

"That's a lot to keep straight. I think I'll just need to try them all. I just wonder how you girls keep such lovely figures with all the pastries and pasta around here. Haven't the Italians heard of low carb?"

"I don't know about that. But I suspect part is genetics and the other part is constant exercise. All the walking. And they tend to eat their bigger meal at lunchtime, in the afternoon, then a light dinner. I guess it balances out," Leah said. "What kind of food do you like? I can pick a place that has something you want to eat."

"If I won't make you uncomfortable, I think I'll just have coffee. I'm supposed to meet a handsome man for lunch after our chat," Joan said smiling.

"Ha-ha, I'm not even hurt that you're passing up lunch with me for a better date. I would choose the handsome man too. Italian?"

"No, Texan." They both laughed as Joan followed Leah into a small neighborhood restaurant. They approached the counter. Leah ordered *risi e bisi* and a soda, Joan ordered coffee, and then they found a small table for two.

"What is *risi e bisi?*" Joan asked.

"It's like the most common meal here, I guess like chicken and dumplings in the southern U.S., it's comfort food. R*isi e bisi* means rice and peas. But it's onion, carrots, and peas cooked in stock, added to risotto with bacon and cheese, in a wine sauce," Leah explained.

"That sounds like heaven," Joan said. A waiter appeared and set a steaming bowl in front of Leah. "And it smells like heaven too. Now I know what I want for lunch."

"Jenna said you were talking to all of us about Kaylee," Leah got to the point. She took a delicate bite of the steaming dish while she waited for Joan to reply.

"Did she tell you what happened to Kaylee?" Joan asked.

"Yeah. It sucks. And murder is a rare thing around here. Venice is a safe place. We all walk around at night. Except for pickpockets, you know. They found a body last year, but they said it was thrown from one of the cruise ships. The woman wasn't a local, and the murder didn't happen here. I'm not sure what to think about this," Leah said.

"Where were you on Sunday night, Leah?" Joan asked.

"I was at a study group. I'm working to try to get a license as a tour guide. We aren't licensed. Which means we aren't legal. That doesn't sit well with me. So, four nights a week I meet with a group of people who are also studying to take the test to get licensed. It's not easy. And it's all in Italian,"

"Have you heard about anyone who would want to harm Kaylee?" Joan asked.

"You think the killer was someone she knows? Not a random event? Or an accident?"

"An accident, definitely not. The crime could be random, but the majority of murders are by someone familiar to the victim. So, we're starting with them. Can you think of anyone?"

## Victimized in Venice

"I hate to say it, but yeah. I can. I mean, I'm not sure he's capable of murder. He seems like a really nice guy, but I guess everyone has a breaking point, and for some people, it doesn't take much. At least, from the television shows I watch anyway," Leah answered. Then she took a bite of her lunch and Joan waited.

"Who are you thinking about?" Joan asked when the girl finished chewing.

"Fabio. He helps out with the study group. He's a Venetian and is a licensed guide. He is angry about all the unlicensed guides. The city doesn't seem too keen on enforcement of that law. He says Venice has seven unlicensed guides for every licensed one. Most of the unlicensed ones give free tours. But you're expected to pay a tip at the end. Most of the time they end up making about the same and sometimes more than the legitimate guides, but because it's a cash tip, the income doesn't get reported," Leah explained.

"If Fabio was mad enough about the unlicensed tours going on, what would make him target Kaylee specifically? I mean, from what I understand, My Venice My Way is more expensive than the local tours, not free. They charge more for the unique native English speakers, right?"

"Right, and that's one thing that makes him mad. Yeah, the free tours tick them off, but the idea that people pay extra for a native English speaker is an even bigger sore spot. Most Venetians think we're responsible for the cost of living increases here because we can afford and do pay more for things. We've effectively made it where they can't afford to live in their city. Like an economic occupation," she said and took another bite of her lunch.

"And you think that would cause him to hurt Kaylee?" Joan asked.

"Oh, no, probably not. Zoe is what would cause him to harm Kaylee," she said.

"Zoe?"

"Fabio and Zoe are engaged. They're getting married on Valentine's Day. But Kaylee told Zoe not to date him. She's been dating him for a year on the down-low, but now the wedding's coming up. Zoe figures she'll lose her job once Kaylee finds out. I guess she doesn't have to worry about that anymore. Now we all have to worry about losing our jobs," Leah said.

"Do you know Fabio's last name?" Joan asked.

"Perna. Fabio Perna. His father is a well-known artisan here. He owns one of the costume shops in town and makes the most amazing costumes and hand-painted masks. We've all been wondering if he's designing Zoe and Fabio's wedding outfits. You know, a Carnival wedding. They won't tell us if that's the case. We're all pretty excited about the event. I think it's going to be fun and amazing. But none of us would have told Kaylee. There are few secrets in Venice, but somehow, Zoe and Fabio managed to keep that one from Kaylee," Leah said.

"Thank you, Leah. Thanks for talking to me, and telling me about Fabio. Zoe wanted us to tell you all that you're all invited to her apartment tonight. She said anytime after five. I think it's so you can all get together and comfort each other over your shared loss," Joan said.

"Shared loss? What happened to Kaylee is sad. No one deserves that. And I feel for her family. But honestly, the biggest loss over losing Kaylee is going to be if we lose our jobs. Zoe was her best friend. I'm sure she's hurting. But the rest of us? Not so much. I hope that doesn't make me seem mean or shallow. She just wasn't someone you got close to if you know what I mean," Leah said.

"Thank you for lunch. I do hope you find who did this."

"As far as your jobs go, you need to talk to Lesley. She's handling everything for now," Joan said.

"Thanks for lunch," Leah said.

## Victimized in Venice

"Thank you! I can't wait to try *risi e bisi* now that you introduced the dish to me. It was nice meeting you," Joan said, and Leah left to walk to her next tour meeting spot.

Joan pulled out her phone and messaged Alen. The time was already two o'clock. She was anxious to meet him, have some lunch, tell him what she learned and find out what he learned too.

*Hi handsome, I'm done. Want to meet for lunch?* Joan texted to Alen.

*Hello, my beautiful bride. I do! I'm near the Liberia Acqua Alta and I've been looking for a lunch spot. So far, the only places open are a pizza joint and an over the top fancy place.*

*I am dying for risi e bisi. I'm sitting in a restaurant that serves it. Want to come here? Or I could get it to go and we could picnic somewhere.*

*I'll come to you. Supposedly it's illegal to eat around town except in restaurants or something. Not sure of the specifics, but don't want to take a chance on it. What's the name of the place where you are, I'll see if it comes up on my phone?*

*Morbido Croccante, on Rugagiufa.*

*Sweetheart, I think that translates to dead crunchy. Are you sure that's where you want to eat?*

*I'm sure you must be wrong. I'll check the translation out while I wait on you.*

~***~

When Alen arrived, Joan showed him the translation on her phone. The restaurant's name actually meant soft crunchy.

Joan told him about her conversations with Leah and Jenna.

"I just talked to Paige. It turns out she and Brandon, one of the guys we're supposed to meet at the bookstore, are dating, and they were in Milan Sunday and Monday. They were both scheduled off for two days and took advantage. Apparently, they both have roommates, so when they're off at the same time, they backpack together to get away. She didn't have anything to offer in the way of a possible suspect. Noah did, though," Alen told her.

"It's sad to say, but it appears her family and Zoe are the only ones who are going to miss Kaylee. It's a shame. She was beautiful and so smart. Especially about business. What do you think made her the way she was?" Joan asked.

"I suppose it could be any number of reasons. It's the proverbial nature or nurture debate, I suppose. This afternoon we talk to Brandon and Blake, the last two employees. And so far, a maintenance guy, a waitress, and Zoe's fiancé are our primary leads," Alen said.

"Well, don't forget that Zach was convinced the killer was an angry tourist. Or a drunk tourist. I can't imagine why a tourist would be angry at Kaylee. Unless they did what we did and took one of the self-guided tours first," Joan said.

"You noticed that too?" Alen asked.

"I did, and to top it off, Jenna told me that Kaylee wrote their scripts and insisted that they recite them verbatim. Your tour too?"

"Yep. Just like the recorded tour. Maybe Kaylee owns the guided tour company too?" Alen asked.

"Oh! That would be an unexpected twist. But wouldn't Lesley know about that?"

"Maybe," Alen answered. "Maybe she just didn't think to tell us. Or that could be Kaylee's little secret. She seemed adamant that her business affairs were private, especially from her family. Maybe she had the other company on the side."

"Lesley said Kaylee had a great mind for business but couldn't be bothered with the financials, payroll, and details. Are you thinking that she had another financial guru or business manager besides Lesley?"

"Could be. Or maybe she didn't have time to do all that for My Venice My Way because she was already doing all the accounting and such for the other business," Alen said.

"As much as I just want to go home and put up my feet after meeting with Blake and Brandon, I'm wondering if we should make an appearance at Zoe's tonight. That might be the easiest place to talk to Fabio," Joan suggested.

"Do you think he'll be at the gathering?" Alen asked.

"They're getting married in a few days. I'll bet he's wherever she is. And now they don't have to keep their relationship and impending wedding a secret anymore. I wonder if she planned the get-together at her apartment instead of a bar or café because the reality hasn't sunk in yet that they don't have to hide anymore?" Joan wondered.

"You know… that might be a motive for murder, right there," Alen said.

"Maybe. But Zoe seems to be the only person who is emotional at all about Kaylee's loss. Hailey cried a few tears, but some people cry over the loss of imaginary characters too. Mostly the reactions have been shocked and surprised more than anything else. So many people seem to have a reason to dislike her. I'm going to bet that it's a Venetian. Tired of her nasty attitude towards them. Not her best friend," Joan speculated.

"You're probably right. We've seen it before, first hand, friends killing friends. But yeah, everyone besides Zoe has seemed more worried about having to find another job than anything else. Let's go visit this amazing bookstore. And you were right. The *risi e bisi* is an awesome dish! I have to learn to make it. This might even be my new favorite. I think it's better than spaghetti."

# Chapter Eleven

"Libreria Acqua Alta means High Water Library. It's a used bookstore with possibly thousands of books from who knows how many centuries," Joan told Alen while they walked to their destination.

"Okay, and do they have a café? What makes this particular book store special?" Alen asked.

"You'll have to see for yourself," she teased as they walked hand in hand. The crowds and walking traffic were noticeably heavier now than when they first arrived, just as Joan's research had predicted. It wasn't as frustrating to be slowed down by the crowds as she thought it would be because about twenty-five percent of the pedestrians were now in Carnival costumes. In another day or two, playing I Spy with the eighteenth century to present day characters would be a great way to spend the day. Thinking about sitting in the park watching them pass by, Joan thought of Carina at home.

"Poor Carina. I thought we would take her everywhere we went while we were here. I hate that she's stuck at home alone," she said to Alen.

"Sweetheart, Carina wasn't aware you had big plans for her. It appears that stuck at home is her favorite place to be. Remember how she glared at you that day, thinking she missed the cat? I think she's okay. We'll go home and walk her when we finish here," Alen said. "Then if you want to go to Zoe's, we can. Did you get the address?"

"Umm, no. I didn't. Do you think Brandon or Blake will have it? And that they will tell us? No one has asked for the address. It seems they all know where she lives," Joan answered thoughtfully.

"Well, we can ask Brandon and Blake. But asking them will ruin the element of surprise if you were counting on that," Alen answered.

"Darn, you're right. I wonder, is there any such thing as a telephone book in this town?" Joan asked perplexed.

"Why don't you call Lesley, quickly. Since she does the payroll and has all the company records, she might have the address. If she does, we don't have to ask. And if she doesn't, we'll ask," Alen suggested.

"Thanks! I would have thought of that. Eventually. It's nice working with a seasoned detective," she said. Then kissed him on the cheek before she dialed Lesley's number. They were almost to the bookstore, so they stopped while she made the call.

She hung up and said, "Success! She's sending the address to my phone. Let's go check out this bookstore," she said. Alen noticed her step was light and perky. She was having fun.

The bookstore wasn't at all what Alen pictured. In his mind, he was envisioning a typical bookstore from the States. Bright lights, carpeting, wide well-marked sections with soft seating, coffee, and gifts. This was a narrow bookstore, with books stacked literally to the ceiling. Most of the titles were in Italian, so he couldn't tell for sure, but it appeared at least in some areas the sorting wasn't by genre, or author name, or Dewey decimal, but by the color of the book. They barely had room to walk.

The flooring was old tile. And occupying the majority of the center aisle was a gondola. The gondola was full of books. Against the walls were shelves that appeared to be built on top of pallet-like structures, not unlike a boat dock. They spied a couple of bathtubs filled with books. And everywhere Alen looked, it seemed, cats were sleeping on piles of books. Joan led him to the stairs. On the wall in English was written, "*Follow the books steps go up*". And sure enough, the steps were built with stacks of books. The books looked like they'd seen better days. Many were missing their covers and, on closer inspection, looked water damaged. At the bottom of the stairs were two large wooden ship's wheels.

Joan was snapping photos. The stairs turned out to be mostly an optical illusion They didn't lead to a second floor or a rooftop view. They weren't even as tall as Alen. In fact, when he was standing on the third step, his head and chest were towering over the wall. The scene made for a fun picture, though.

"They certainly have made interesting use of the space," Alen said laughing. "It's so small and tight, I would have never thought of trying to fit a gondola in here. And bathtubs are certainly a different means of display," Alen said. "Looking for books in them kinda feels like digging for movies in the three-dollar bin at the big discount store in the states."

"There's a reason for it," Joan said. Multiple times a year, Venice floods. The tides rise, the city is sinking and the water comes in. Look, here are some photos with the water outside higher than the door. So, the valuable books, they put in the boat and the tubs to help protect them from the floodwaters. They call that *acqua alta,* which means high water. If you've noticed the metal frames and sheets of plywood in the alleyways, they lay those down when the water rises for everyone to walk on."

"Okay, so this place just went from gimmicky and touristy to brilliant. What would I do without my research hound wife?" Alen asked.

"You would probably be sitting in a recliner in Texas watching television and wondering if you were going to grill sausages or hamburgers for dinner," she teased.

"That was just mean," he said, laughing. They made their way back out of the bookstore. There clearly was no place to meet up within the bookstore.

"Luckily for you, I was researching the neighborhood when you called earlier," he said, "And I saw someplace close by to go and talk to the guys when they get here. I can do research too. I just prefer to see things with my own eyes instead of searching the internet," he said.

"Great! What's this place called?"

"It's a pizza joint called Peter Pan Pizza," he told her.

Joan laughed.

"What?" he asked.

"Are you serious?" she asked.

"Yes, why would I make that up?"

"Here we are in the heart of Venice Italy, and we're going to a place called Peter Pan Pizza. You just gotta love this life," she answered. Alen still wasn't sure what was so funny.

"Technically it's Peter Pan Pizzaria," he clarified.

"That's so much better," Joan said, tongue in cheek, but the actual name did make a little more sense to her.

Joan noticed the now-familiar striped shirt on a young man approaching from their left.

"Here comes one of them," she said to Alen.

"The other one too," he said, nodding to their right.

They introduced themselves and agreed to go have a seat and a snack at Peter Pan's. Alen ordered their drinks and a pizza to share while Joan, Brandon, and Blake decided on a table outside under an awning.

"I assume by now you both have heard about Kaylee?" Joan asked.

"Yes, madam," Brandon said in a light British accent.

"No, what happened to Kaylee?" Blake asked.

"Mate, she met a sticky end," Brandon said.

"What does that mean?"

"She was murdered on Sunday night," Alen said, serving drinks off a tray to them all and sitting down.

"That's terrible," Blake said.

"We are wondering if either of you saw her on Sunday evening?" Joan asked.

"My girlfriend and I were in Milan on Sunday and Monday," Brandon explained. "You already talked to Paige and we were together."

"I was at my girlfriend's house on Sunday evening. Technically, it's her parent's house. I was there for Sunday evening dinner with the folks. Her name is Alma. She's Italian," Blake offered. Joan noticed he was getting more nervous.

"Do either of you know anyone who would want to harm Kaylee?"

"No, I didn't know her that well. She seemed nice enough the few times I was around her, but I've heard stories that she could be mean as a jungle cat, given half the chance," Brandon answered.

"I never even met her. I talked to her on the phone when I answered an ad," Blake said. "Look, I just found this job. I've only worked for the company for a week. It took me three months to find a job. I was so excited. I want to ask Alma to marry me, but I need a job. Am I going to have to find another job?".

"I don't think so. But you'll need to talk to Lesley. Do you have her contact information?" Joan asked.

"Yeah, of course. She's the only one I ever talked to before. I figured out all the rest of the guides are friends at some level. But this is the first time I sat down with another employee from the company. Hey, I thought we weren't supposed to be together with our work shirts on. I thought it was weird that Lesley said to meet you guys and wear the work shirt," Blake said.

"It's a unique situation. Wearing your work shirts was so we would recognize you," Joan answered.

"So, who are you guys?" Brandon asked.

"We are house sitters. We're house-sitting for Kaylee's dad and stepmother. And we're just helping out in a difficult time," Alen said.

"Good. You almost come across like cops or something," Brandon said.

Alen and Joan looked at each other and smiled.

Alen said, "I was a sheriff before I retired. And it seems like my wife was an undiscovered Sherlock Holmes. But you shouldn't worry about that. Just eat some pizza, son, and be happy."

While they polished off the Italian pie, Joan told them both about the gathering that night at Zoe's.

When they parted ways, Alen and Joan decided to take the water bus, or *vaporetto*, home to walk Carina. Thanks to the late lunch and the slice of pizza, neither one of them would be ready for dinner for a long while.

While they walked in the park with Carina, they discussed plans for the next day.

"I was planning to take a class tomorrow. Pasta and Tiramisu from ten to one. Will that work with your plans?" Alen asked Joan.

"I will make it work! As usual, I love that you're learning to cook. Even though these days, it doesn't feel like we're home much to cook. My favorite part of our new lives is me not having to cook dinner every night," she said.

"I know. And I remember we said we were committed to doing new things. I'm learning to cook all kinds of fun stuff. But I'm worried that you aren't getting to do new things. Is there anything I can do to make that happen for you?"

"I'm doing new things. I'm talking to strangers. Investigating crimes. Walking dogs in exotic locations, eating new foods. Going to festivals. All of it is new to me. I'm enjoying taking photos and making travel videos. I'm perfectly happy. I'm challenged. I'm never bored. It's a great life we chose, and I'm still thrilled we decided to leave our routine lives behind and do this,"

"What were you planning for tomorrow? As far as tours or whatever. Will my class interfere?"

"No, I didn't have anything on the list, except the Carnival opening ceremony parade tomorrow evening. But we can watch the parade from the comfort of home. The windows in the living room open up over the Rio di Cannaregio, and the parade will pass right under them."

"Okay, we've been here less than a week, and you have no tour scheduled? That's not normal," Alen asked concerned.

"Well, there are tours. But I figured out you weren't enjoying them. Other than the Casanova experience and Carnival, I didn't find much in the way of weird quirky stuff like you enjoy. Most of the tours are more about the city, the architecture, and all the pretty stuff. I want to talk try to talk to the waitress, Gisella, and maybe the maintenance man tomorrow. I could do that while you're in your cooking class. Then we could have dinner at home and enjoy the parade. What do you say?"

"I don't like that idea at all. I realize I shouldn't feel this way. But you could be confronting a murderer. I prefer you not to do that alone. And yes, I would feel the same way if you were a man," he answered. "Could we talk to them together after my class? We should have plenty of time to do that and get home before the parade."

"Okay, I understand. And I never feel like you think I'm inferior in any way except experience. I can take another of the self-guided tours and take photos, or one of the photo walking tours while you are cooking," she answered.

"Or you could have a relaxing day at home. Read a book. Take a bath," he suggested.

"No. Not yet. I can't relax until we figure out what happened to Kaylee. When we get home tonight, we need to check with Zach and see what's going on and if the cops have given them any more information," she said.

"Yeah, that's a good idea. I feel like he'll contact us when he learns anything. But checking with him isn't a bad idea. I haven't wanted to mention this. But if Ray and Holly aren't coming back until after Kaylee reaches the U.S., we may be here longer than we planned. That sometimes takes weeks or months to do," he said.

"Oh, no! Alen we are obligated to house sit for someone else. We can't leave them in a lurch. What will we do?" Joan asked.

"I don't know, but we'll figure out how to handle the situation," he said.

"I was so excited to spend Valentine's in Venice with you and our anniversary in another country," she said.

"Me too and it might still happen. Let's get Carina home and go see what's happening with the young people at Zoe's."

# Chapter Twelve

JOAN AND ALEN EXITED THE elevator on the fourth floor and heard music. When they looked in the direction of the music, they saw one door open wide, and they recognized the attendees. They walked in that direction, certain they had found Zoe's apartment. Just as they approached the door, the group around Zoe's living room raised champagne glasses.

Hailey said, "Here's to us and the next chapter. May Dame Fortune ever smile on us, but never her daughter, Miss Fortune." Six people raised their champagne glasses, clinked them together, and said in unison, "Cheers!!"

Leah said, "I give you play days, heydays, and paydays!"

The group toasted with "here here!" and "cheers" again.

Noah said, "Here's to turkey when you're hungry, champagne when you're dry, a pretty woman when you need her, and heaven when you die." He raised his glass to Hailey and winked when he said a pretty woman. The group laughed and toasted again.

A handsome man, big, strong, and fit with Mediterranean coloring, said, *"Chi non è impaziente non è innamorato,* which means he who is not impatient is not in love."

Alen and Joan realized the speaker must be Fabio. The group cheered and toasted again.

Zoe said, "May the tide of fortune float us into the harbor of content."

The last person to toast had her back to the door. Joan thought there was something familiar about her but couldn't place her as one of the employees. As soon as she spoke, Joan realized who she was. She was shocked that she was at this apparent party.

Lesley said, "May the saints protect you and sorrow neglect you, and bad luck to the one that doesn't respect you."

After the toasts, Zoe said to Fabio, "Could you open another bottle, please? We are all dry. We can have no more toasts."

The big man went off, presumably in the direction of the kitchen.

Joan knocked on the open door to alert the revelers of their presence.

"Joan, Alen! Welcome! I didn't think you would come," Zoe said, then called out after Fabio, "Amore! Bring two more glasses. We have more guests."

"Thank you, Zoe. I have to say, I've never been to a champagne wake before," Joan said surprised.

"Oh, yeah, I guess this does look bad. But it's not a wake. We are all celebrating coming changes. I'm sad, truly sad, that Kaylee isn't here with us. But life goes on," she explained.

Fabio returned with two glasses of champagne he carried perfectly in one hand, and a bottle to refill everyone else's glasses in the other.

"In Italy, we believe that when someone dies, they don't want to leave," Fabio explained gently. "Especially when someone dies too young. We bury them with their favorite things to take with them so they don't need to return, and we don't speak of them. We believe this allows them to cross peacefully to the other side."

"Lesley, I was surprised you were here," Joan said.

She looked a little sheepish. "Zach is home with the girls. I came in to meet with Fabio and Leah about the future of My Venice My Way. Honestly, I wasn't ready to go home. Zach is so distraught. I wanted to celebrate the future without feeling guilty that the reason we have great new plans is the source of his pain," Lesley answered, using care not to use Kaylee's name in front of Fabio, to honor his culture.

"I see a few of you are missing. Have you heard from them? Are they coming later?"

"No, it's just us tonight. Jenna never hangs out at night with us. She works with her family until she falls into bed, and none of us have met Blake yet. Though I hope to get to know him and his girlfriend Alma soon. They will be the other cross-cultural couple in our group," Zoe said.

"Brandon is in the process of moving out of our apartment and in with Paige," Noah said.

"Okay, then. Tell us what you're all celebrating. We'll celebrate with you," Joan said.

Noah said, "As soon as Brandon gets his smelly stuff out of my apartment, the lovely Hailey has agreed to move in with me," he said beaming at the girl across the room.

"As roommates or as a couple?" Alen asked confused.

"As my one true love," Noah said sappily while everyone laughed.

"Congratulations," Joan said. "I didn't realize you and Brandon were roommates, nor that you two were dating."

"No one knew until tonight," Hailey explained.

"Fabio and I can finally enjoy the last few days of our engagement openly. I realize I was wrong to keep our engagement a secret. But now we can celebrate and share our excitement about the wedding coming up in a few days," Zoe said.

"Leah and Fabio are going to work with me to make My Venice My Way legal!" Lesley said, excited. "They will help everyone pass the licensing exam. I think in the long run, that will please Zach too. He loves this country and we've been talking about trying to get citizenship. Me owning an illegal business, even though we skirted that by being a foreign entity, just seems wrong. So, we were celebrating that too. I'm sorry if this was shocking to you or seemed disrespectful at all."

"No, don't apologize. When in Venice… Right?" Alen said.

Alen had planned to try to talk to Fabio. But in light of the Italian tradition of not speaking of the dead, he sipped his champagne and wondered how he could talk to Fabio. He also couldn't help feeling like everyone in this room seemed to have something to gain by Kaylee's untimely death. And in his experience, that meant any of them, or even all of them, could be suspects. Fabio was certainly big enough and strong enough to hurl a body stuffed in a duffel bag into the canal. And from what Joan told him on the walk over, Kaylee's apartment was very near here. He tuned back into the conversation going on around him when he heard Joan speak again.

"You guys, have the Polizia talked to any of you?" Joan asked.

They all looked around the room at each other as they all shook their heads no.

"Hmm, that's weird. I would have thought they would have started with her employees," Joan commented.

"You have to remember, these guys are kind of off the radar because the company is. We are registered through the government as a foreign operating entity. But that's in Rome and we aren't required to register here in the city," Lesley reminded them.

"That makes sense," Joan said.

"Also, I think it's human nature for them to explore all possibilities that are Italian speaking first. It's easier," Zoe said.

Alen made up his mind. He didn't want to offend anyone, but he felt the room was brimming with people who had both motive and opportunity. If the local police weren't investigating this crowd, he owed it to Ray, Holly, and Zach to do so.

"Fabio," Alen said, "I wonder if you would mind taking a walk with me and showing me around the neighborhood?"

"With pleasure," he answered. He kissed his soon to be bride and walked to the elevator with Alen.

"I sense you have questions for me. It's okay. I'm happy to answer them."

"I understand your tradition and don't want to offend you," Alen said.

"No worries. We won't use her name. We understand who we are talking about without using her name, which might summon her back to this place. What do you want to ask?"

"Could you show me where her apartment is? Was? Joan said she thought it was near here. Someone told us she had a problem with a man working in her apartment. We are planning to try to talk to him tomorrow, and if I knew where the building was, finding him tomorrow would be easier," Alen said.

"Certainly. I have never been to her apartment, but I do believe it's close. If you don't mind, I need to call Zoe and find out exactly where the building is," Fabio explained.

"Okay, that's fine," Alen assured him.

"I know it's this direction, we can start walking," Fabio said as he dialed his phone.

"Amore, I'm going to show Alen how to find the apartment of your friend. But I'm not sure exactly which building," Fabio said and then listened. "*Gratzie*, we'll be back soon," he answered before disconnecting the call.

"We are set now," Fabio said to Alen. "I know where to go."

"You speak very good English. Where did you learn it?" Alen asked.

"I studied in school. I started in lower secondary and continued through upper secondary and also at University. I also lived a semester in Ireland. My parents were adamant that we all learn a second language if we wanted to stay in Venice. Tourism is our main industry here and being multilingual is very important," Fabio explained.

"Do you understand the phrase the elephant in the room?" Alen asked.

"I do. And I suggest not only an elephant in this room. There is a whole safari. Ask your questions," he said.

"Someone told us that you are a licensed tour guide here. And there are possibly seven times as many who aren't licensed. I'm sure that creates some animosity between the two groups. Did you have a personal grudge against, umm…" Alen stumbled.

"Her. Did I have a grudge against her? I did. But not for the reason you are thinking. Yes, as a group we are resentful of those unregistered. Not so much because they take business from us. There is plenty to go around. But because they aren't licensed, they sometimes provide bad experiences, which makes us all look bad. And because they don't have to pay the local fees and taxes, they can make more money with less work. She did work to provide a good experience. I can say that for her. Even if she did steal the talking points from another company. That company is also a foreign operator, so whatever," Fabio explained.

"My grudge against her was about Zoe. She was Zoe's best friend. But because of her prejudice, she actually had the audacity to forbid Zoe to date me. For a year, since the company started, we have dated in secret. For three months, our engagement has been a secret. And that's bad enough. But what hurt me most was that the woman I love wouldn't be able to have her best friend at her wedding by her side. Supporting her, not only during the wedding but for the rest of our lives. She made it clear, that Zoe would lose her job if she dated me. We knew as soon as she discovered we were wed that would be the end of Zoe's job and her friendship. The job was no problem. You see, we are full of secrets. Zoe is already a licensed guide. She was just still working for My Venice My Way to stay close to her friend as long as possible. But we were both mourning the coming end of the friendship. Much like knowing a friend has a terminal disease. So, you see, we've understood the end was coming. In a way, this is easier. Now, she won't bump into her friend who turned her back on her around the city. But if you are wondering, I did not cause that girl harm. That would have been causing Zoe harm too, and I can't do that. Here's the building," Fabio pointed. "She lived on the top floor."

"Okay, you've convinced me that you didn't have anything to do with the murder," Alen said. "Do you know anyone who might have been more willing to harm her?"

"That list is many, my friend. Her problem was not just her business, but her attitude. Are you familiar with Niccolò Machiavelli?" Fabio asked.

"I am, of course," Alen answered.

"Machiavelli once said, everyone sees what you appear to be, few experience what you really are. She, who we are discussing, did not follow that example. She rarely hid her true feelings about anything, nor her deplorable behavior. When I was living in Ireland and when I've traveled to other countries, I felt I was a guest in someone's home. I tried to be respectful of that, and I think most travelers are. But she was not. It was as if she thought the whole world should be like her home. And she had no tolerance for differences. Many people speak of karma. Especially in a situation like this one. But I think in this case, Machiavelli also inspired the killer. He also said if an injury has to be done to a man it should be so severe that his vengeance need not be feared," Fabio said. "As for if I know of someone specific you should look into, I can't think of anyone. I'm sorry I can't help more."

"Thank you for showing me the apartment, and for speaking so frankly with me. Joan and I wish you and Zoe a lifetime of happiness. And success in your new business venture too," Alen said and clapped Fabio on the shoulder. He liked the man.

"Will you and Joan still be here for Valentine's Day?" he asked in the elevator on the way up to Zoe's apartment.

"We will," Alen answered.

"You are invited to our wedding then. We would be honored for you to attend. Zoe can get you the details," he said as they walked into the apartment, where the gathering had progressed from toasts to a dance party.

Joan was ready to go home. It had been a long day. And Carina needed one more walk before bed. Hopefully, the potty outing would be short and uneventful.

"This case is very frustrating. It feels like everyone who knew her or had any dealings with her had a problem with her," Alen said.

"The her is Kaylee?" Joan asked.

"Sorry. Yes. When Fabio and I talked of her, we only referred to her as she or her, not her name, to respect his beliefs of not wanting to call her back to this realm," Alen explained.

"Well, what do you think? Do you think he did it?" Joan asked as they walked home.

"No. I don't think he has the chops for that. He's a nice guy, very philosophical, and very in love with Zoe. His biggest problem with Kaylee was not how she treated the locals or her illegal business that was competing with his or that she intimidated Zoe into hiding their relationship, engagement, and impending marriage, but that Zoe would have to do those things without her best friend. He says they've already been mourning her loss for some time, certain she would walk out of Zoe's life as soon as the marriage took place," Alen said.

"That's sad," Joan said. "You know, a lot of people seem to be benefitting in some way from her death. It looks like Fabio, Leah, and Lesley will take over the company, make it even better, and maybe all of them make even more money. Zoe and Fabio don't have to keep secrets anymore. Zach will have more money for his affordable housing project. Holly and Ray won't have the embarrassing temper-tantrum- throwing daughter they are supporting. That's more money in their pockets too. And then we still have the angry waitress and the verbally abused maintenance man. And in all of this, with all these people, we found no love interest. No boyfriend, no ex-boyfriend. How many beautiful young women do you know that don't date?"

"That's an interesting question, my love. And it's so un-PC and 1990's of you. Haven't you heard? Women don't need a man to make it anymore? Many women elect to seek education and build a career before muddying the waters of life with often distracting and messy romance. And then there's the possibility she was in the closet about something. She could have been a member of the trans, asexual, or homosexual populations. Maybe she was in one of those and keeping the relationship secret. Who knows? I say we don't need any more suspects!" Alen said.

"Right this minute, part of me wants to say, this isn't our barbeque, not our coleslaw. Let the police figure this out, and let's just enjoy Carnival," Joan said, surprising Alen.

"Really? It's okay with me if you want to forget all this. And darn it! Now, with all this great Italian food around that we still need to try, you've got me craving barbeque," Alen said.

"No, not really. I can't walk away from a mystery. I just need a good night's sleep. And maybe my handsome young chef to make some barbeque spaghetti for dinner tomorrow," she teased.

"Hmm, that's not a bad idea, we were going to stay in tomorrow night and watch the parade. Why don't I wait here for you to come back down with Carina and we'll finish this long day? I want to cuddle with my wife."

## Chapter Thirteen

SUNRISE WAS SLEEPY ON THURSDAY morning and a gentle rain was falling when it was time to take Carina for her morning constitutional. Neither Alen, Joan, nor Carina seemed to mind too much. Bundled up in rain gear, they set out for the park.

"It doesn't look like a very good morning for a photography walk unless this rain blows out of here soon," Joan said.

"You could have a morning at home. A long hot bath, read a book? Then…"

"Alen, haven't you figured me out better than that by now? How could I sit at home, in my pajamas, under a quilt, curled up with a dog, reading a mystery novel, when we have a real mystery underfoot?"

"Indeed, how could you?" he answered, resigned.

They walked along in silence, both thinking. Once Carina was done with her business, they stopped at the corner bar and ducked inside for a warm croissant and a hot coffee for breakfast.

"I could get used to this," Joan said.

"What?"

"Morning walks, sweets or heavenly bread and coffees for breakfast. Though, I'm beginning to wonder if Venice would become too small over time. While it's beautiful here, I'm starting to think dry land would be nice. Roads and cars."

"Well, Mrs. Arny, what do you propose to do this morning while I'm in cooking class? Or shall I cancel my class? I could play hooky with a hot sleuth…"

"No! Don't cancel your class. I might do a little research and planning online. I want to plan a special Valentine's celebration for us."

"I was planning to do the same," Alen said. "But we've been invited to Zoe and Fabio's wedding that day. I don't have any details yet like the time or anything. Maybe we can make a day of celebrating love. I'll plan an activity, you plan an activity, and we go to the wedding."

"That sounds like the perfect way to spend the day of love, in the city of love, with the one I love," Joan said.

Alen looked at her out the corner of his eye. She knew her name was about to tumble off his tongue before he even opened his mouth.

"Joan Michelle Arny, that is undoubtedly the corniest thing you have ever said!"

"Right? I couldn't resist. Kiss me!"

When they got home, Alen took his shower first. Joan started research on the computer. When he joined her at the kitchen table for another cup of coffee, he smiled at the frog table runner. They had not had much time in this place to enjoy the simple things.

"I was looking for a self-guided tour I could take today because it's stopped raining," she said. "But at first, everything I was finding sounded like something you might enjoy."

"Hmm, like what?"

"Well, there are walking street food tours," she said.

"Yes, please."

"I found a bar hop tour, visiting bars for cocktails and appetizers,"

"Yes, please," he answered again.

"What about a Carnival mask treasure hunt where you have to find clues and solve mysteries?" she asked.

"That sounds like fun if we ever find the clues and solve the mystery we already have," he said.

"Do you feel the same about the ghost and legends night tour? It says, hear about murder, mystery, and more on a night tour of Venice."

"When are we going to do all these tours? We only have nine more days here. Assuming Holly and Ray can return on time. Did Lesley mention if they have any news about when they will release the body?"

"Okay, then. That solves it. After my shower, I'll call Zach and see if he's learned anything new. Then, if necessary, I'll try to figure out what to do if we can't leave, but we need to be at the next house-sitting gig. I can call the House Sitting Academy and see if there is a protocol for this sort of thing. And if I have time left, I'll just roam around and take some photos. Maybe of the opera house and whatever else I find, until time to meet you. Fortunately, Kaylee's building and thus the maintenance man and the restaurant where Gisella work are in the same neighborhood. Maybe we could just meet at London Chips and have lunch while we try to talk to Gisella. What do you think?"

"Honestly, I think I want to try some more local dishes," Alen answered. "But I want to wrap up this case and enjoy the rest of our time here. So, I'll meet you at London Chips between one and one-thirty. While you're in the shower, I'll be looking into some Valentine's ideas until time for me to leave. Do you want me to make another pot of coffee?"

"Yes, please. The cloudy skies are making me sleepy."

Dressed and ready to go, Joan sat down on the sofa with her phone prepared to call Zach. To her surprise, Carina hopped off of her usual throne by the window and jumped onto the couch with Joan. She circled a few times and then laid down against Joan's thigh making as much human to fur contact as she could.

"Aw, baby girl. I'm sorry we were out last night. We missed you too. We'll be home with you tonight. We'll watch the parade together out the windows, okay?" she said stroking Carina's back, scratching behind her ears and under her chin. Carina sighed a heavy sigh as if to say, okay.

Then Joan called Zach with the phone in one hand, and the other resting on Carina's back. Both the lady and the dog receiving comfort from each other.

"Zach? It's Joan Arny. How are you?"

"Hi, Joan. I'm sorry I haven't talked to you guys in a couple of days. I'm okay. Is everything okay at the penthouse? Is Carina okay? Are you and Alen okay?" Zach fired off without taking a breath. His voice was still uncharacteristically quivery too, Joan notice.

*This man is on the verge of breaking down,* she thought.

"Zach, everything and everyone here is fine. We're all okay," she said calmly. "I just called to see if you or Ray has heard anything else from the police? About Kaylee's case, or when you'll be able to send her to Ray in the U.S."

"Oh, thank goodness. I'm relieved everyone is okay. The police won't talk to me at all. Even though Ray told them they could and I speak fluent Italian. It's very frustrating. But we don't know anything yet. I've made all the arrangements I can without knowing when they will release her. All the paperwork is done. Ray thinks they said we should have a day's notice before they release her. As for the case, they say they are talking to several persons of interest. But that's all they will say."

"Okay, that's good," she assured him. "Is there anything we can do to help you? Do you and Lesley need anything?"

"No, thank you for asking. We're just waiting. I'm going back to work today. Lesley says she has the tour business under control.

## Victimized in Venice

One of the girls is helping her out. She thinks today it will be back to normal at our house with Avery and Brenna. I try hard not to say things like, nothing will ever be normal again. And I'm trying hard not to panic and pick up my girls and move away. The city is overflowing with so many strangers, and now I don't trust any of them. Between the tourists and the cruise ships, will my daughters be safe here? And if we leave, where should we go?" he said, sounding like a man spinning out of control.

"Zach, honey, calm down. Your girls aren't actually living in Venice. You're in a quiet little town on the mainland, and I'm sure your girls are perfectly safe. Bad things happen everywhere. No place can guarantee you nothing will happen to people you love. This is life. You have a calling here. You have something you are passionate about here. Lesley seems excited about continuing with the tour company. Your mother is here. Running to a new place will not solve anything. Do you know only eleven percent of all murders are random acts committed by strangers? It's almost always someone that knows the victim. That can happen anywhere," she told him.

"Thank you. That helps. This is a weird feeling. I can't get it out of my mind. I don't know what to do," he said, sounding much calmer and also very tired.

"I understand. That's normal. None of us like feeling helpless and most of us have no experience to draw on in situations like this. And that's where we are right now until we can understand what happened and why. Then you will be able to think more reasonably. That would be a better time to think about changes or decisions about your family. Not right now, okay? If you or Lesley need anything, just give us a call," she reminded him.

"Thank you. Have a good day. I hope you're enjoying your visit," he said before disconnecting.

Joan looked down at Carina. "Boy, Carina, your brother Zach is really freaking out. I hope we can solve this soon. I'm going out for a while. I need to take some photos and go for a long walk. It's going to be a lot of walking, but do you want to go with me?" she asked. Carina looked up at her and Joan thought the dog appeared to be thinking about it and trying to decide. She sighed a big sigh again, stood up, hopped off the sofa and went back to her chair. Not toward the elevator.

"The queen has spoken," she said to no one in particular and grabbed her raincoat and her camera bag on the way to the elevator.

~***~

Having consulted her map, Joan began walking toward the famous Venice opera house. She had read about it on the internet and knew it was called *Teatro La Fenice*. *La Fenice* means the phoenix. The original theater was called *Teatro San Benedetto* and was lost in a legal battle in the mid-18<sup>th</sup> century. The Noble Association of Box-Holders decided to build a new, bigger, better theater and name it the Phoenix. The name turned out to be prophetic. In 1774, 1836, and 1996 the theater was destroyed by fire. The latest fire was arson. Each time, the opera house was rebuilt. The story reminded Joan of her conversation with Zach. And how many families had to rebuild after tragedies. Tragedies born from the loss of a vital family member, homes lost to acts of god, financial crises. She realized we are all works in progress, we are all phoenixes, always rebuilding.

The front of the opera house, the façade, the only original part remaining after the last two fires seem extraordinarily plain to Joan. It was a white flat building absent of the typical decorations and design features of many of the other buildings around Venice. There was a single dentil molding around the top. But once she stepped through the doors into the foyer, Joan began a tour into opulence she had never experienced before. Marble floors and stairs illuminated by crystal chandeliers and two wide staircases led her into the theater. She was struck with the elegance of a room that appeared to be made of gold, five tiers of boxes up the sides, a painted ceiling, and the feeling that great musical history had been born on this spot of the earth. It felt almost religious. She snapped photos, wondering what they would

## Victimized in Venice

look like and if any photo could ever capture the magic that seemed to lie under the great domed ceiling.

Joan decided at that moment that she wanted to experience the Leonardo Da Vinci Museum. She wasn't as disappointed in the façade of this building; it was more decorative and ornate than that of the opera house. She felt she had stood on reverent musical ground that morning, and now she wanted to see some of the finest art in the world. Inside, Joan fell in love with the museum. They displayed high-resolution digital images of the most famous of Da Vinci's paintings, and they were backlit, highlighting loads of details. They did this because there was no need for security and visitors could get as close to the paintings as they wished, studying the most minute details in the paintings. They exhibited not only the famous drawings of his engineering mechanical concepts, but also the built machines constructed from the drawings. They even had a virtual reality lab where she could watch the construction of the designs. In this city that at times seemed stuck in the eighteenth century, this modern age museum won the prize for how to spend a fascinating morning, Joan thought. But she lost track of time. And when she left the museum, she realized she needed to hurry to meet Alen on time.

The walkways, alleys, and bridges seemed teeming with people. Even more of whom were in full Carnival costumes and masks. But looking out into the canal, the water traffic seemed even slower than the foot traffic. The water buses and taxis had people crushed together so tight they seemed to be hanging over the sides. She decided walking would be better.

She felt like she was being carried through the crowd as if she was on a people mover at the airport. The whole crowd seemed to move as one animal. Someone was touching her on every side. She tried to not crowd the person in front of her. But the muscles of the huge beast wouldn't allow it and pushed her forward closing all open spaces.

And then someone whispered in her ear.

"Mind your own business or go back where you belong. Your life depends on it. Do you understand?"

Joan tried to swivel her neck to see who was talking to her. She tried to stop moving. But the force of the bodies around her kept propelling her in forward motion. Until they reached a corner. She knew that the creepy whisperer was wearing a Carnival costume, she knew it was red, and she knew he was wearing a white wig. He was behind her but slightly to the right of her, and she could get glimpses of him out the corner of her eye.

When the crowd reached a corner, curving to her left, she was pushed around the corner toward the inside and the man behind her was pushed to the outside. She could see he was in a full-face mask. She tried to pay attention to as many details as she could as he pushed and shoved to get through the mass in front of him and eventually disappeared from her view.

When she arrived at London Chips, Alen was waiting for her in front of the restaurant.

"I was beginning to think I might be stood up," he said.

"I was accosted by Casanova," she answered.

"That wily rascal. He's been dead over two hundred years and still has a way with the women," Alen said thinking that Joan was teasing him.

"No. Really. I was threatened by a man whispering in my ear while wearing a Casanova costume," she explained.

"Wait! Threatened? What do you mean threatened?"

"He said to mind my own business or go back where I belong," she paused, wondering if she should continue or not, and then remembered how she hated secrets between them she continued, "He said my life depends upon it."

"Do you think you would recognize him if you saw him again?" Alen asked concerned.

"No. Not even a chance. But if he was pressed up against my back I might…" she teased trying to lighten Alen's mood.

# Victimized in Venice

"What?"

"It was crowded. Really crowded. I've never experienced anything like it. It was like the crowd moved as one being. Anyway, he was behind me. And in a costume with a full mask. I might recognize the costume, but there are probably hundreds of the same costumes floating around Venice this week," she explained. "It might even be rented."

"You seem pretty calm considering," he said impressed.

"I've had a great morning. And I'm with my husband now. We're going to crack this case; I just feel it. I can't be bothered by a creepy whisperer who gets his jollies from trying to frighten women in a crowd. It was probably a hoax anyway. I mean who here would care what I was up to? Except for Kaylee's killer and he wouldn't have any reason to know who I am. I just thought it made for a fun excuse for being late to meet you," she said.

"Well, that's one way to look at it, I guess," he said unconvinced.

They found one empty table at the back of the restaurant. Much to their dismay, their waitress was named Amber, not Gisella. And she had a British accent, not Italian. Which made Alen wonder.

They both ordered fish and chips, something they loved when they were in the U.K. in Edinburgh and London. And then Alen turned his attention to Joan.

"This whisperer. What kind of accent did he have?" he asked her.

"Oh, I haven't thought of that. Well, he was whispering. So, you know, the whole breath in the ear, shiver and cringe thing was going on. He did speak English. He did have an accent. He wasn't Texan for sure. Maybe he was from the Midwest?" she questioned.

"Joan, sweetheart, could you take this seriously for a minute? It might be important. What if he was Kaylee's killer?"

"Honestly, Alen. What are the chances of that? He had an accent, but I couldn't identify with any degree of certainty where it was from. At least not at a whisper, it might have been British, or Italian, or Bangladeshi for all I could tell," she said, clearly done with this conversation.

She was busy scanning the crowd. Looking for her prey, an Italian waitress named Gisella.

Their waitress Amber brought their lunch, asked if they needed anything else and then scurried off to serve her other customers. The restaurant was packed. Joan remembered two cruise ships were scheduled to arrive in Venice that day and realized that accounted for a lot of the extra bodies all over town. Joan balanced eating, keeping a lookout for the waitress they wanted to talk to, and talking with Alen about his cooking class.

"What did you learn to cook today, honey?" she asked him.

"*Gamberi alla busara,* which is prawns in tomato sauce, *Gallina Ubriaca,* which means drunken hen, and tiramisu," he answered.

"Mm, those sound yummy. Are you making one of those for dinner tonight?" she asked.

"Well, I probably should, since it's the official kick-off of Carnival. Or lasagna which is the main Carnival dish, because, in the early days, people couldn't afford to buy the cheese to make lasagna but once a year, so they only had it during Carnival. But I still have your idea for barbeque spaghetti in my head. I have everything I need at the penthouse to make a chicken spaghetti in barbeque sauce, so I think that's what I'm going to do. It's funny how just learning to make a few things translates into being able to figure out how to make more things," he said.

"Oh, oh, she's coming this way!" Joan said. "I can read her name tag."

Alen was momentarily confused about who was coming towards them. Between thinking about cooking and Joan's encounter with Casanova still buzzing in his subconsciousness, Alen had forgotten the reason they were eating in this particular restaurant.

Joan was surprised. For some reason, in her mind, Gisella was going to be a young lady. But she wasn't. Joan guessed she was in her late thirties to early forties.

"She's much older than I thought she would be," Joan said softly, just barely above a whisper. She wasn't even sure in Alen could hear her over the noisy crowd.

"Maybe she's the senior waitress or head waitress," Alen suggested also speaking softly.

"You know, that makes it even more admirable that she's trying to learn English. It's harder as we get older to learn another language as you and I are discovering. She's probably got kids at home to take care of too. And I bet in her day, they weren't teaching English in school like when Fabio was in school," Joan said.

"The problem is, this restaurant is so busy, there is no way she can stop working and talk to us. I think we need to find out when her shift ends," Alen said.

"How are we going to do that? Just ask her? Did you see how fast she moved past our table? She looked very determined to get wherever she was going. She doesn't strike me as one who will stand around and chit chat," Joan said.

"Amber seems chatty enough. When she comes, we'll ask her when Gisella's shift ends," Alen said.

"Hmph, I would have thought of that. In another minute," she said. Then smiled at Alen and added, "It's a lot more fun solving crimes with you. I loved London. I'm confident I can do it on my own, but it is more fun with a partner."

"And safer too," he mumbled, still concerned about Casanova. He didn't think it was as likely to be a benign encounter as Joan was.

They found out that Gisella's shift didn't end until 5 p.m., and Amber said the restaurant was likely to stay just as crowded until then.

"Let's go see if we can talk to the apartment maintenance man, Lapo, and then we can come back," Alen suggested. "Luckily it's all in the neighborhood. What time does the parade start?" he asked.

"At seven. We have some time. Let's go see if we can get any information from Lapo," she agreed.

# Chapter Fourteen

THEY WALKED AS THEY USUALLY did, hand in hand to get to the building that Fabio showed Alen the previous evening. It wasn't a comfortable stroll like they were used to, it was crowded. This area wasn't as bad as the tourist area Joan walked through to get to the restaurant from the museum, but the crowd dictated their pace, and it wasn't as quick as either of them hoped.

When they arrived at the building, they discovered that the door was locked. On the wall outside the door was a panel featuring six doorbell intercom buttons. Each one had a sun-faded number on it, but no names. Alen started with the top left and rang a bell. He waited for about a minute. When no one answered, he rang the next one. Eventually, he rang the last one. They waited. They were about to decide that no one was home in the building. Since most Venetians work and the city was so crowded, feeling like everyone in town was out walking about, it didn't seem too strange. They were about to walk away when someone answered. They couldn't tell from which bell they had rung or apartment, but at least someone was home.

"*Buongiorno*," came the male voice reply through the speaker box.

"*Buongiorno*," Joan answered. "*Lei parla inglese?*"

"Yes, I speak English. Who is this?" the unidentified speaker answered.

"We are looking for Lapo Muni. But we aren't sure what his apartment number is," Joan answered.

"He doesn't live here. He moved out," was the reply.

"Thank you, have a good day," Joan answered. She turned to Alen. "Now what?"

"It looks like the chances of me cooking dinner tonight are diminishing. The woman who owns the building is a British woman named Sophia Porter. Noah said she can be found every night at Harry's Bar. After we talk to Gisella, we will have to see if we can find Sophia and if she has a forwarding address for Lapo. We have a couple of hours to kill before we can do anything. What would you like to do?"

"We need to go home and walk Carina early. Then come back out. We can't predict how late we might be getting home with all the Carnival hoopla tonight. We'll be walking for sure. I think most of the taxis may shut down during the parade," Joan answered.

"Great idea. I'm glad you thought of Carina. She's a good dog. Let's go take her for a walk."

~***~

Alen and Joan arrived back at London Chips at 4:30 p.m. It was less crowded than when they were at the restaurant a while earlier, but it seemed like a new dinner rush might be starting to filter in.

Amber greeted them at the door and didn't recognize them.

"Could you seat us in Gisella's section, please?" Alen asked.

"Gisella is not working the tables anymore. Her shift is almost over," the waitress explained.

## Victimized in Venice

"Oh," Joan said disappointed. "We were hoping to talk to her when her shift was done. Is there someplace we could wait for her? Or could you tell her we're here?" she asked sweetly.

"Yes, I'll tell her you're here. What are your names?"

"That won't help much. She doesn't know us. But we need to talk to her about someone we know," Alen said.

"Okay, I'll tell her. You can wait over there. I'll be right back," she said and disappeared in the direction of the kitchen.

In a few moments, the waitress was returning but stopped to seat a group of six people before she returned to them. When she did, she had good news as far as Alen and Joan were concerned.

"Gisella said she doesn't have much time. She has to go home and get her children ready for Carnival festivities. But she'll be out to talk to you in a few minutes," Amber told them.

"Thank you," Joan said. They sat on a bench waiting for the lady they saw earlier. She spoke softly in the direction of Alen's ear so she wouldn't be overheard.

"I don't think Gisella is our killer," she said.

"Oh, why not?" he asked.

"If she is, she couldn't have done it alone. She's older, heavyset, and while I'm sure she's a hard worker, and carrying trays of food would build upper body strength, she doesn't strike me as strong enough to manipulate a body into a duffel bag and hurl it into the canal," she pointed out wisely.

"Do you remember how much trouble you and I together had to get the bag out of the water?" Alen asked her.

"Yes, that's why I say, I don't think this is our gal," Joan said.

"Well, there are two extra factors here. It's easier to drop something into the canal then to pull it up out of the water. Also, it was wet, which adds more weight than when it was dry. I'm not disputing what you're saying. Honestly, it would be difficult for any person to accomplish unless there was a lot of adrenaline involved. Which there likely was. I think you're probably right. We are probably looking for someone younger and more physically fit, but you can miss important facts if you discount a suspect for any reason," Alen reminded her. Gisella approached them, curious but wary.

"*Ciao*, how can I help you?" she asked in English, spoken slowly and deliberately.

"*Ciao*, Gisella. Some friends of ours told us you might be able to help us. Do you know a young lady named Kaylee Roberts?"

"No, I do not know that name. But as you see, I serve people many all days. I do not learn the names. I are sorry I cannot help you," she said in broken English.

Joan pulled off her backpack and unzipped it. She pulled out the framed photo of Kaylee from the Roberts' spare room and showed it to her.

"Aye yai yai, si. I know her. We call her *brutto Americano*! It means the ugly American. She is infamous in Venice. Mean," Gisella said.

"When was the last time you saw her, Gisella? Our friends told us she was very rude to you," Joan said slowly, watching Gisella to see if she appeared to understand what she was saying.

"Si, that girl is terrible. I understand you. I understand English. I just have a hard time remembering it well. I lived in the United States for a while when I was young. But I went years many I not speak it. I forget many things. It's been a long time since I seen brutto Americano. Maybe two, three weeks. She was only here at the night hours. I only work night hours two or one night a month. I can see the sche… uh, calendar. One moment, please," she said and went back to the kitchen.

Gisella returned with the work schedule to show them it had been three weeks since she worked the night shift.

"Do you know where she lives?" Joan asked.

"No, I don't bother with her. She is known to all the Venetians as the *brutto Americano*. But I do not care about her life. I have family and work. No time for bad children. Why? Why are you asking about her?" Gisella asked.

"Something happened to her on Sunday night. She was murdered," Alen said.

"*Mio Dio, riposare in pace*," she said and crossed herself as a good Catholic would do. "You are here because you think I hurt that girl? I have a daughter her age, I couldn't harm someone just because they spoke ugly words."

"Thank you for talking with us, Gisella," Joan said. "Do you know anyone who might hurt her?"

"No. Venetians are easy people. We say Italian proverb, *Il modo migliore per ottenere lodi è morire*. It means the best way to get praise is to die. No one speaks bad about the dead. If we kill someone bad to us, they will only be remembered as good. I do not think an Italian kill that girl. I have to go home now to my children," she said.

"Thank you, again. I hope you and your family enjoy the Carnival," Joan said.

Joan and Alen followed her out of the restaurant. She went right, and they went left to find their way to Harry's Bar. It had been on Joan's list of places to go, as the most famous bar in Venice, the one where celebrities hung out when they were in town. Nearly every person they passed was in costume. And the walkways were just as crowded as they had been all day.

"What's our plan? How will we recognize Sophia Porter in the bar?" Joan asked. She was aware if she had known ahead of time, they would need to find her, she would have tried to search for her on the internet and get a picture. But Sophia had been on Alen's radar.

"I wonder how many people will be in the bar with a British accent?" Alen wondered aloud.

"I would say a fair few. Is that our only information about her?" Joan asked.

"Sweetheart, you're a great sleuth. And you're much better than me about researching the internet about a lot of things. But I am well versed in how to find people," he said. He pulled out his phone and showed her a photo.

"At first when I searched, I found a beautiful young woman, but she's famous and lives in New York, there are a lot of Sophia Porters it turns out. But this one is from the U.K. and lives in Italy," he explained.

She was an older, white-haired lady.

"She's beautiful and has lovely skin," Joan mentioned.

The crowd was getting so thick they couldn't continue to talk. Alen put his phone securely in his pocket and grasped Joan's hand so they wouldn't be separated. They focused on finding their way to the bar.

They clearly were early for the crowd at Harry's Bar. They saw no sign of the white-haired lady they sought, so they took a table and ordered Harry's famous Bellini cocktails.

"I've been thinking and what Gisella said makes a lot of sense. And maybe it's the clue as to why there are so few murders here," Joan said.

"About only speaking praise for the dead?" Alen asked.

"Yeah. It would certainly be a deterrent to killing someone out of anger," she said. "And it makes me wonder if we're barking up the wrong tree spending any time looking at Italians. I realize you've been suspicious of Lesley and some of the others all along, and I hated to think of any of them being capable of this. But maybe we have to revisit that," she said.

"There's just one thing that bothers me about that," Alen said. "Fabio said they don't speak of the dead, and Gisella said they only speak fondly of the dead. Those statements are incongruent," Alen said flatly.

"Oh! You're right," Joan said, more intrigued. She sat and thought for a moment.

## Victimized in Venice

"That's the thing about proverbs," Joan said. "They often contradict each other. For instance, the early bird gets the worm and good things come to those who wait," she pointed out.

"You make a good point, my lovely bride. The crowd is arriving," he said. "But it appears we are grossly underdressed. With all the wigs and masks, I wonder if we'll recognize Sophia," he said.

A cocktail waitress arrived at the table to serve their Bellinis.

"Are you looking for Dame Sophia?" she asked.

"Yes, is she here?" Joan answered.

"No, not yet. That is her table by the window. She is here every night. Are you supposed to be meeting her?"

"No, we just wanted to talk with her and we heard this was her usual spot. We haven't met her yet," Alen said.

"Okay, when she arrives, I'll tell her you would like to speak to her. She's very friendly. Especially if you buy her a drink," the waitress said with a smile and a wink.

They enjoyed people watching until she arrived.

"So much for our home-cooked dinner tonight," Alen said.

"There's always tomorrow, my love," Joan said.

"I have lovely plans for Valentine's Day. But we do need to find out the details about Zoe and Fabio's wedding if you want to go. It doesn't matter to me if we go or not," Alen said.

"I have ideas too. But you're right. I can call Lesley and ask her for details. Maybe in the morning. It's getting too loud in here to hear on the phone now," she yelled across the table to him.

He just nodded in response.

A woman dressed in costume, but not the more typical 18th-century dress approached the table. This woman was dressed in an elegant burgundy velvet flapper dress adorned with sparkling sequins, a gold embroidered neckline, and long hem fringe also in gold. She wore black elbow-length gloves and a black boa around her arms. Her legs were covered in black fishnet stockings and she wore gold high heeled sandals. She had long dark brown hair, almost black, and a gold headband with a tall burgundy feather. Joan admired her. She had the body to make the costume look both sophisticated and sexy.

"I heard you dolls were looking for me?" she cooed in a British accent.

"Are you Sophia Porter?" Alen asked.

"I am, no sense in denying it, I guess. Everyone in here knows me. What can I do for you?"

"Can we buy you a drink?" Alen asked.

"I thought you'd never ask," she answered.

Alen stood up quickly and pulled out a chair for her, offering her a seat. He motioned for the waitress.

"Thank you," Sophia said. The waitress appeared with a cocktail in hand.

"Your usual, Dame Sophia. You look dashing tonight," the waitress said and scurried off to wait on other patrons.

"She's right. That costume is something extraordinary, and I suspect you make it even better," Joan said surprising herself. Joan was not a clothes horse, not a girly girl, and except for an extremely rare occasion in London recently, she couldn't remember the last time she wore a dress.

"Thank you, my lady," the older woman said.

"Dame Sophia," Joan asked, picking up on the woman's preferred name, "we're looking for Lapo Muni. We understand he lived in an apartment building you own and recently moved out. Did he leave a forwarding address by chance?"

"Oh, that lousy, backstabbing, little jit? No, he and that little American girl ghosted me," she said.

"Do you mean Kaylee Roberts?"

"I do indeed. That girl ran me ragged with every little dustball needing attention. So, I made a deal with Lapo, half-price rent to keep her out of my hair. The rent comes due and both of them have vanished. I suppose he took it literally when I said to keep her happy. Anyway, now I have two empty apartments. You in the market? That little spoiled brat left everything in hers, though. I'll rent it to you furnished," she said.

"Kaylee didn't run off with him. She didn't abandon the apartment. She was murdered," Alen said.

"I'm so sorry. That would explain why she didn't pay the rent and left everything." After a brief pause, she continued, "Now I feel bad. Other than constantly whining and complaining she was a good tenant. She always paid her rent on time. She was quiet, I shouldn't have jumped to that conclusion. She gave no reason for that. It was just coincidence I guess that Lapo disappeared at the same time, oh! That's why you're here. It's no coincidence at all, is it?" she asked.

"We don't know. We heard she had a running argument with Lapo, which is why we wanted to talk to him, and now his disappearance does appear suspicious. Do you know anything about him? Is he from Venice, does he have family here, a reference, anything like that?"

"Okay, he might not have been the soundest business decision I ever made. No, I don't know anything about him. He approached me offering handyman services in exchange for small living quarters. I was desperate. I made the deal with him and forgot about it. Oh, dear. What if he's a serial killer or something and I led him right to her door? That would make me responsible for her death, wouldn't it?" she said, motioning the waitress for another drink.

"The only one responsible for Kaylee's death is the person who killed her," Alen said wisely. He'd been in this situation before where innocent people took on the guilt of a crime by association.

"Thank you for talking to us," Joan said. "If you think of anything that might help us find him, would you call us?"

"I will. But I don't have any information that can help you. I did have him fill out an application with references and I let him move in. I admit it was a couple of weeks before I checked any of the references. None of the phone numbers worked. I think they were all made up. But by then, Kaylee wasn't calling me every day to complain, and I just let it go," she said. "It was very stupid and irresponsible of me."

"Don't beat yourself up too much. There's nothing that can be done about it now, except to try to find justice for Kaylee," Alen said.

"I do hate to speak ill of the dead, and I do hope the police find whoever did this and they pay the price. But that girl had a lot of enemies in this town," Sophia said.

"Is there someone in particular we should talk to about her?" Joan asked.

"No. I've lived here for a long time. A lot of Venetians have forgotten I'm not from here. I hear them talk. They call her the ugly American. I certainly never heard anyone threaten her or anything. But, as I said, she paid her rent on time and was quiet. I minded my own business about everything else," Sophia said.

"Thanks again, we'll let you get back to your evening," Alen said.

Alen paid the check, and they decided to start the walk home with the idea they would stop along the way for appetizers or a pizza for dinner.

"It's another dead end," Joan said sadly.

"Maybe it's time we talk to the police and share with them what we found. They will have means to try to track down Lapo," Alen suggested.

"You mean tell them what we've learned about all her employees too? Alen, we were just suspects in a murder that we didn't have a thing in the world to do with just because we were foreigners. I sure hate to offer up innocent people. Remember that case here in Italy a few years back where an American college girl was charged with murder. I think she was in jail for around four years before she was acquitted. I don't want to be responsible for that happening to anyone," she said emphatically.

"Yeah, you're right. I forget not everywhere has the same laws that I was used to. But we could tell them about Lapo," he said.

"What if we tell Zach about Lapo and let him tell the police. To be honest, I would prefer to stay off their radar," she suggested.

"That's a good plan," he answered.

On the way home, Alen and Joan couldn't help but get caught up in the festivities. They walked along the canal watching the decorated boats with their costumed passengers in the opening parade. Street vendors were out on every corner it seemed selling *fritole, crostoli, favette,* and *galani,* the famed pastries of Carnival. Alen and Joan sampled it all. Almost sick from the sweets, they stopped at the neighborhood pizzeria near the penthouse and ordered a pie to go.

They went home, threw open the shutters and watched all the activities from above. Carina was glad they were home. When things started to die down, they took Carina for her last walk of the day.

"We are out of leads, aren't we?" Joan asked.

"Maybe not. Sometimes it's beneficial to talk to people a second time. Sometimes their stories don't match up. I would like to say, yeah, we've done all we can, let's just play Carnival for a while. But I have an idea," Alen answered.

"What? Or should I ask who?" Joan asked.

"In the morning, we should call Zach and tell him about Lapo. And we need to ask Lesley about Zoe's wedding. We also need to figure out how we're going to handle things if Holly and Ray don't make it back in time for us to make our next commitment, though, I think I have that figured out. But then, I think we should talk to Leah and Fabio. It seems too convenient to me that they are going to go into business with Lesley, taking over Kaylee's company less than a week after her death," he said.

"Okay, that's our plan for tomorrow. You're probably right, but I hope it's too obvious to be true. I so didn't want this to be about the business. I especially hope Lesley didn't have anything to do with it," she said before they both fell asleep.

SCARLETT MOSS

## Chapter Fifteen

AFTER CARINA'S MORNING WALK WITH Joan and Alen's breakfast stop, Alen called Zach. Joan had told him how frantic and nervous Zach was when she talked to him the day before.

"Good morning, Zach. It's Alen Arny. How are you?"

"I'm doing better. Joan talking to me yesterday helped. I still haven't heard anything yet about when Ray and Holly will return. Did they message you?"

"No, we haven't received anything from them, but under the circumstances, we didn't expect to hear from them and don't want to bother them. Joan and I are going to figure out today what we'll need to do if they can't get back when they planned to because we have another house-sitting job lined up for when we leave here. But that's not for any of you to worry about. We won't leave Carina or the house until they get back," Alen told him.

"Thanks, Alen. We all appreciate that. But we have been talking about it already. We realized we could bring Carina to our house if you need to leave before they get back. I realize you guys probably already have airline tickets, not to mention the commitment you already have," he said relieving Alen.

The only solution Alen had come up with was for one of them to stay in Italy and the other one to go on to the next location. With Joan's Casanova experience, he didn't want to leave her alone here in Italy. But if he had learned nothing else about this house-sitting business, one never knew what to expect in each new place.

"The reason I called was to pass on some information we discovered in case you want to share it with the polizia. Honestly, we don't want to interact with them if we can help it since we aren't family and I don't know how they would react to us snooping around on our own. It's up to you what you want to do with the information," Alen said.

"I certainly understand that. Plus, it's easier for Lesley or me to talk to them since we're fluent. What did you find?"

"We learned that Kaylee's landlord made a deal with a guy named Lapo Muni. She gave him a hefty discount on renting an apartment in the building in exchange for handyman services and upkeep on the building. Some of Kaylee's employees told us that she and Lapo did not get along well and we discovered last night that he vanished. When the landlady went to collect the rent, he was gone with no notice," Alen told him.

"That certainly seems suspicious, doesn't it?" Zach asked.

"It might be a coincidence but might not. Dame Sophia had him fill out an application, but when she tried to call the references listed, none of the numbers work. She thinks they were made up. I figure the police probably have a way to track him that we don't," Alen said.

"That does sound like information I should pass on to them. And maybe if I'm providing information, the flow will come back to me too. Thank you, Alen. I appreciate this. Do you have any other suspects or ideas?" Zach asked.

## Victimized in Venice

"No, so far, other than Lapo, we feel like we've run out of leads. But we'll keep trying of course," Alen said.

"Hey, this isn't your job. It's the job of the local cops. We appreciate the help, like I said, especially telling all the employees so we didn't have to, and her landlady. I haven't thought that I probably need to pack up her apartment too. But you and Joan should be enjoying the city and the festivities. I didn't mean for you to be working this," Zach said.

"It's okay. It's our pleasure to help. But we are going to get out and try to have some fun. We're trying to plan a special Valentine's Day since we're in the city of love," Alen told him.

"That sounds great. And if you need anything at all, be sure and call us," Zach said.

"We will. I think Joan is going to call Lesley to get details about Zoe's wedding. Fabio invited us to attend. We're thinking a Venetian wedding on Valentine's will be pretty spectacular," Alen said.

"Yeah, Lesley has all the details. We're planning to go too. I think it'll be an event. Fabio's father is one of the premier ateliers in the city. He makes the most extravagant costumes, and from what I've heard, he is creating all the clothes for the wedding party. Going to this wedding will be like being on the set of a movie. Oh, hey, speaking of movies, the film crews are here to film some scenes for the new *Mission Impossible* movie. You might run into Tom wandering around the city if you're lucky," he added.

"I'll tell Joan and we'll keep a lookout. I bet she would love to get photos of that. Thanks for the heads up, we'll talk soon," Alen said before disconnecting the call.

Alen knew Joan was upstairs talking to Lesley at the same time. He decided to make some coffee they could enjoy together while sharing about the two phone calls.

When Joan came down, she had all the details about the wedding. It would be in the afternoon at a venue called the Glass Cathedral on the island of Murano, one mile north of the city of

Venice. Period costumes were encouraged though not mandatory for the guests. After the ceremony, there would be a sit-down meal and then a dance party with disc jockey that was expected to run into the evening. Lesley had assured Joan they could go for all or just part of the wedding activities if Fabio invited them. Lesley also told her that Fabio's family was one of the most prominent in town and she felt there would be no expense spared for a fairy tale wedding. Joan was excited about attending and thrilled that Holly and Ray had costumes they would borrow for the event. It was shaping up to be a fun Valentine's day. She also had Lesley's spreadsheet of contact information and addresses for all the My Venice My Way employees. They could use it to get in touch with Leah to set up a meeting and hopefully she would have Fabio's contact information and he could meet with them too.

Once Alen shared with Joan about his conversation with Zach, they decided they were ready to contact Leah and try to set up a meeting. Joan found she was as excited about the wedding and possibly running into the American film crew as she had been about Carnival. While she still was enjoying seeing all of the elaborate costumes, she found the crowded throng of people exhausting.

After phoning Leah and setting a time and place to meet her, Joan called Fabio's number that Leah gave her. He explained that he was working that day and the only time he could meet was either his lunch break or after work. The café where they were meeting Leah was convenient for him to meet them on his break, which was before they were supposed to meet Leah. It was decided they would meet Zach at eleven and Leah at twelve-thirty. If the two overlapped, it would be okay.

~***~

"*Ciao*, Fabio, thank you for meeting us. Can we buy you lunch?" Alen said, shaking the man's hand.

"Yes, thank you. It's my pleasure to meet with you," he said sitting down.

## Victimized in Venice

A waiter appeared and took their order. They ordered a large platter of assorted cicchetti to share. It included *tramezzini*, which were tea sandwiches. Three varieties of the finger sandwiches were one with tuna, olives, and capers, another with asparagus, tomato, and boiled eggs, and the third had bresaola, a type of cured beef, with parmesan and arugula. Also, on the platter was the Venice famous *Sarde en saor*, which were deep-fried sardines that were marinated, and *polpettines*, which were small fried balls made with meat and potatoes.

"I sincerely do hope you will come to the wedding," Fabio said.

"Yes, we are delighted and honored to be invited. I got the information from Lesley this morning, and we can't wait to attend your special day," Joan said. "I imagine you are very busy these last few days. It sounds like the wedding will be a fabulous affair."

"I am not busy at all. My parents and Zoe's parents are doing all the work. All we have to do is show up. We're pretty excited about it too. I want our wedding to be Zoe's most perfect day of her life," Fabio said.

"We wouldn't miss it," Alen said.

"Fabio, we asked to meet with you, hoping that you can explain how it will work with My Venice My Way, now that you are joining the company and Kaylee is gone," Joan asked him.

"Oh, si, yes, first we will change the name and a little of the premise. I will help train the guides so that they can be certified and licensed like I trained Zoe and Hailey. It's best if they can speak Italian. The exam is in Italian. But to rush the process, I will teach them what they need for the exam with the hope they will continue to learn. We will offer the tours in a variety of languages, not just English, and we won't make it so obvious that the company caters to native English speakers. This should broaden our customer base," he said.

"Have you settled on a new name?" Alen asked.

"No, not yet, but we are thinking something like Your Venice, Your Way. It keeps the same feel without being so possessive," Fabio answered.

"How long has this partnership been in the works?" Joan asked.

"Just since the day before yesterday. Lesley came to bring the payroll like she always does. Everyone wanted to know about the future of their jobs. She said she and Zach were talking about if she thought she could manage the company on her own. Her biggest problem, of course, would have been picking up tours if someone was sick or couldn't work for some reason. With her little girls at home and living almost an hour away, it could be problematic if someone canceled at the last minute," he explained.

"And you have a solution for that?" Alen asked.

"I think so, yes. I think if we open up to all the markets, we can employ more guides. Most of the locals speak at least two languages. I have friends and acquaintances, legal guides who speak Spanish, German, even Japanese. Many of them speak three languages which means we have more people we can schedule in an emergency. Once everyone is trained, of course," he said.

"What were your and Zoe's plans before Kaylee died, when you thought Zoe would lose her job?" Alen asked.

"She was already hired by the company I work for. She is supposed to start when we return from our wedding trip. But we were planning to save money to start our own tour company. Now, we will go into partnership with Lesley and Leah instead. There is no investment start-up money needed this way, just to share expertise and work hours," he explained.

"I'm sorry, but I have a shorter lunch break than my friends and I have to return to work now. I look forward to seeing you in a few days. I hope this helped you in some way," Fabio said, clearly confused with their questions.

After he was gone, Alen said, "I'm convinced he didn't have anything to do with Kaylee's death. He is an intelligent man, and if he was guilty, he would not have been confused about our questions."

## Victimized in Venice

"I agree. Alen, I love these little balls of meat and potato. What are they called?"

"*Polpettine*," he answered.

"Can you learn to make these too, please? I might follow you anywhere and do anything for a dinner of these," she teased.

"For you my queen, I will learn," he promised.

When Leah arrived, they asked her nearly the same questions and were satisfied with similar answers.

For now, Alen and Joan felt they had done all they could do to find Kaylee's killer.

Suddenly they heard a lot of commotion and yelling. Most of the yelling was Italian, and Joan and Alen didn't understand.

Alen found a waiter who spoke English.

"What's going on? What's happening?" Alen asked him.

"There is a very bad virus. It's on the news. Some people tested positive in Venice, so the government is shutting down everything. Everyone is supposed to go home. And what we ask. We are still hurting from the floods in November, and now the government canceled Carnival! They close the schools, universities, museums, and tours. The cruise ships will not come. Venice will sink for sure, not into the water but into debt. We are doomed. All the tourists will leave now," he complained, blaming the government for taking precautions.

"I'm so sorry," Joan said.

"Be very careful. We understand the virus is dangerous. But for us, we wonder what is the point of living to only starve to death, or not be able to pay our rent," he said before walking away.

Alen and Joan had read about the new virus that started in Asia. But they never thought about being trapped because of it.

"I think we should head home and see what we can learn on the news," Alen said sensibly.

"Yes, let's go. Maybe we can think of who else might harm Kaylee too. We'll have an easier time talking to people if they aren't working," Joan said.

SCARLETT MOSS

## Chapter Sixteen

WHEN THEY GOT BACK TO the penthouse, Joan booted up her laptop. The news was bad. Italy had gone from a handful of cases to hundreds of cases overnight. Italy was now considered the European hotspot for the Covid 19 Novel Coronavirus, a cousin to MERS and SARS.

"Oh dear, this is bad. There are cruise ships with infected people, and no one wants to let them dock. People are canceling airline and hotel reservations all over the world. I guess we shouldn't get so consumed with our stuff and forget what's going on in the world, huh?" Joan said.

"We have an email from Ray and Holly too. They've decided to come back and not wait on Kaylee to get to the U.S. They are afraid they won't be able to come back and we won't be able to leave," Alen said.

"Well, darn! What does this mean? We're going to miss Carnival. The grand ball we were going to attend was supposed to be tomorrow night. Now that's canceled. Are we going to miss

Valentine's Day, and the wedding too? And where will we go? It's a relief that we won't miss our next commitment, but what if they cancel their trip because of this too?" Joan asked.

"Let's not get too excited until we see what's going on. I'm sure even if they get back tomorrow, Ray and Holly aren't going to kick us out in the street. And if they do, Zach and Lesley would probably take us in. If what the waiter predicted comes true, there will be thousands of vacant hotel rooms here. We're going to be fine Joan. There is no need to panic," Alen said.

"I'm not panicking, I'm pouting. We're going to miss all the fun stuff," she said.

"I bet you all the money in our bank account that wedding doesn't get canceled. It sounds like a lot of time, planning, and money has been spent. And if they do have to cancel it, we'll find a way to have our special day," he said consoling her.

"I guess we get to have our dinner at home tonight," she said.

"It will be my pleasure to cook for you," Alen said.

"I can take Carina for her walk," Joan said. Maybe I can snap a few photos of costumed beings running for their life or something,"

"You girls have a nice walk. I'm going to sit down and write some notes about the interviews we've done about Kaylee. I feel like I'm missing something. I should have been making notes all along. And then I'll prepare dinner for us. If you go buy the produce market near the park, will you get the makings for a salad to go with our pasta?"

"Sure. Come on girl, let's go for a walk and see what's going on out there."

Alen made a list of each of the people they interviewed in the case. He was trying to remember something. Once he had a list, he visualized each meeting and tried to recall all of the conversations. There was something he was forgetting, something that slipped through the cracks. He was sure of it.

## Victimized in Venice

Joan and Carina went to the park. A large number of people were still scurrying around. They all looked in a hurry. Joan decided to take a seat on one of the park benches where she would watch the pedestrian traffic and speculate where everyone was going. She had to admit that it felt good to just sit down and enjoy her surroundings. She was wondering if this new virus was something they needed to be concerned with or if the government here was just being extra cautious. The decision to cancel Carnival and not allow the cruise ships to dock was going to be a blow to the city and the business's already troubled incomes as well as to the citizens who would lose a lot of work. She was thankful she didn't have to worry about that for her and Alen, but she wondered if it would affect their travel plans. She decided she was going to contact the next homeowners and see if they were considering changing their plans.

Then she saw him. At least she thought it was him. It was the same costume, she was sure. Casanova was walking briskly through the park. Few people sitting in the park and not many were even passing through. She knew she had to act fast. Wishing that Alen was here with her, she had to make a decision. Should she follow him or hide from him. She decided she couldn't be a sleuth if she was that afraid. It was still daylight after all.

"Come on, Carina. I think I saw a cat over there. How fast can you move, girl?" she whispered to the dog.

The overweight bulldog was not a good partner for a foot chase. All she could do was try.

The Casanova look-alike must have felt her eyes drilling into his back because something made him look back over his shoulder. When he saw Joan he picked up his pace and walked much faster. He took a path that was overgrown with low lying tree limbs, and she lost sight of him.

She and Carina were picking up speed, but she knew they wouldn't catch him. Still, she followed to see where he was going. If he was going home or to a business, it might lead them to him. But realizing that he recognized her and picked up speed confirmed that it was the same man that whispered a threat into her ear. A threat she was still grappling to understand.

Her heart was racing, she was pretty sure Alen would be downright angry about her pursuit. Ducking under the branches that obscured her view of the path, she discovered that the walkway led to an iron gate. It looked closed, but it wasn't latched. She opened the gate to find it opened into an alley outside of the park. She and Carina trotted as fast as the short-legged dog could to the end of the alley. They passed two side alleys but Joan's gut told her to keep going ahead. It opened up onto a busy thoroughfare with shops and stores lining both sides and crowds of people walking.

She lost him. She turned back to retreat through the alley back to the park and realized they had run right past a small café table with two chairs. It had been empty when they ran past. But now a man was sitting in one of the chairs. A woman came out of a doorway with an awning overhead and joined him in the other chair. When Joan reached them, she paused.

"Do you speak English?" she asked.

"Yes, we're from America," the woman answered.

"Did you see a man run through here a moment ago in a Casanova costume?" Joan asked. Carina sat next to her panting.

The couple both laughed. The man answered Joan.

"You're kidding, right? Everyone in this town is wearing a Casanova costume except the three of us and the pooch there. We even saw dogs in costumes today on the Rialto bridge. Darndest thing I've ever seen," he mused.

She realized the doorway the woman came out of looked like it opened to a hotel lobby.

"Is this a hotel?" Joan asked.

"Yes, it's very nice. We recommend it," the lady said.

Joan tugged on Carina's leash and crossed the narrow alley to peek inside. There was a bar or restaurant inside and she was excited

## Victimized in Venice

to see a large crowd gathered there. They all had on costumes. She decided she should be safe enough in the hotel, and she picked up Carina and walked inside.

She approached the doorway to the restaurant and scanned the crowd looking for a red costume. She spotted a couple, but upon further inspection, none of them had a white-haired wig on, and she realized her guy wasn't there.

"Okay, Carina. I guess we lost him. We better go home and tell Alen about this. He's not going to be happy," she muttered to the dog.

She set Carina down and they began their walk home. When they got to the produce tents, she remembered she was supposed to take home the ingredients for a salad. She stopped to buy what they needed. It was still early and she was surprised to see many of the vendors were closed up already. She found one that was still open, but with little produce left to sell. She wanted to ask why everyone was gone, but she didn't have the Italian language skills to do anything but to point at what she wanted to buy.

She managed to get a small bundle of rocket lettuce, one tomato, two large carrots, three stalks of celery, and a tiny avocado. It would have to do. It was all the seller had left. She wondered if the other stalls were closed because they sold out too.

When the elevator doors opened, Joan called out, "Alen, we're back."

She assumed he was in the kitchen, so she unhooked Carina's leash and hung it on the hook near the elevator door and walked toward the kitchen.

"You won't believe what happened," she said. But when she reached the kitchen it was empty. There were no signs of any dinner cooking either. She placed the bag of salad produce next the to sink and went in search of her husband.

She found him in the room where their computers were. He was on his laptop typing probably ten words a minute with only his index fingers. It was impressive what he could do with two fingers.

"Honey, what are you doing? I called out when we got home," she said.

"I'm sorry. I remembered. I finally remembered what it was that we forgot," he said excitedly.

"We forgot something?" Joan asked confused.

"Yeah. We forgot about the self-guided tour company. Does Kaylee own that too, and if so, does she have other employees, and if she doesn't own it, is someone angry because she plagiarized their material? And I also realized, we should be poring over the travel review sites to see if any unhappy customers left bad reviews for My Venice My Way. If a customer was mad enough to commit murder, I bet they would leave bad reviews," he said.

"Great. That's good news. We have more options now, maybe we'll find more suspects. Alen, I saw Casanova again," she said seriously and plopped down on the bed behind the desk where he was working.

His fingers stopped their mad assault on the laptop keyboard and he turned in his chair to look at her.

"The same one? Was it the same costume, or do you think it was the same guy? Did he say anything to you?"

"I'm pretty sure it was the same guy. I started following him, and when I did, he started walking away as fast as he could walk. I guess he didn't want to call attention to himself by running. I lost him in an alley. But no, he didn't say anything to me this time. But I'm wondering, was he in the park because he was following me or does he live or work in the neighborhood? Was it a coincidence? Should I be afraid?" she asked concerned.

"I think you should have been afraid before you followed him into an alley. That could have ended badly. What were you thinking?"

"I had Carina, the guard dog, with me," she said.

"Oh, yeah, and how funny would it be if I had to tell Ray and Holly I lost their dog too? What if something happened to you?"

## Victimized in Venice

"Okay, I understand I did a stupid thing, maybe. You don't have to beat me up. I was just trying to see where he went. There was no way with Miss Chubby and Lazy down there we could seriously chase anyone," she clarified.

Alen stood up from his chair and walked over to her. He held out a hand and she took it. He pulled her up to standing, wrapped his arms around her, and squeezed her in a tight hug.

"I'm sorry," he said. "So, I guess something new for me is that I have to get used to you being in dangerous situations. That's going to take some getting used to," he said. He was calmer now.

"We are all home now. Everyone is safe. But it feels weird out there. I can't put my finger on it. Everyone seems to be in a hurry. And all the produce tents appeared to be sold out and shut down. I bought a few things to make a small salad, and it was the last produce there for today anyway," she told him.

"Why don't you bring a laptop to the kitchen. You're even faster at research than I am. I'm trying to find out who owns the self-guided tour company. I found their website where you buy the tours, but not who owns the company. You can research, and we can brainstorm all this while I cook dinner," he suggested.

"Good, I'm getting hungry," she said.

"Hey, that's my line…" he retorted.

In the kitchen, she opened her laptop.

"The name of the phone app is called WiseTours. The logo is an owl with binoculars. But I suppose the company could have a different name than the app," she said.

"Yeah, the website says WiseTours by Great Pond Logistics. I did a search for Great Pond Logistics, and I didn't find anything," he explained.

Joan's fingers were flying over the keyboard.

"Talk to me and tell me what you're doing, Sweetheart," Alen said.

"Well, I know you searched, but just to be thorough I searched Google, Yahoo, and Bing for the company name. Now I'm searching the member directory for the Better Business Bureau. It would be much easier if we know what country they are located in. It's a crapshoot that they are a U.S. company, but I know places to search there whereas I don't have a clue about other countries. Here it is! The operating address is in Delaware and that could be problematic," Joan said.

"Why is that problematic?" Alen asked.

"If I remember correctly, Delaware has some of the strictest privacy laws regarding business owners. If a business owner doesn't want to be found, you won't find them if they're licensed in Delaware. A business there has to have a registered agent. That agent handles all the legal business, tax returns, lawsuits, et cetera and forwards it to the owner," she answered.

"May I ask how you know this?"

"Yeah, one of the girls I worked with at the dispatch office wanted to create a new business to sell her handmade jewelry, but she didn't want her soon to be ex-husband to find out about it. There are other states like that too, I think it's Wyoming and possibly Washington. Anyway, I remember her talking about it," she explained.

"Unbelievable," Alen said.

"What? Men have hidden money from women they were divorcing for decades," she said.

"No, I mean you are unbelievable. Is there anything you don't know?"

"Oh, yeah, tons. But I know how to find out most things I ever need. So, because the company is a member of the Better Business Bureau, they have to provide contact information for a company representative. It doesn't have to be an owner necessarily. The name listed here is Matthew McKenzie. The listing says his job title is customer contact with an email and phone number. With the time difference, it's afternoon there. What do you think? Email or phone call? And what should I say, Sheriff?"

Alen grinned. He'd forgotten the sound of her calling him sheriff. He wasn't even sure when she stopped doing it. Probably when he asked her to stop after he retired. He was in a dark place then following the whole ordeal in Corpus Christi and didn't feel worthy of the title. He liked hearing it again.

"A phone call is usually faster," Alen said. "And it's harder for him to ignore. As for what to say, you can say just about anything. You could say you're a customer. You can use a fake name. You can say you're a private investigator. Whatever role you want to play, just don't say you're law enforcement. I'm pretty sure that's illegal everywhere in the world. What you need is a reason to ask who the owner is. If they registered in Delaware seeking privacy, it might be hard to get that information if you do have a believable and compelling request."

"Hmm, I could say I'm with Publisher's Clearing House," she suggested.

"I said believable and compelling. Does anyone believe Publisher's Clearing House even exists anymore?"

"I dunno. I'm not going there. Can I say I'm a lawyer?" she asked.

"Sure, but that might get you sent straight to the registered agent," he told her.

"A lost Nairobi prince with a huge inheritance I need to give away?" she teased.

"Naw, it would never work. Not on the phone anyway. You don't sound anything like a Nairobi prince," he said.

"How do you know? Have you ever talked to a prince?" she asked.

"Not from Nairobi." They both had forgotten how much fun they had together when they weren't so focused on tragedy and drama.

"Okay, seriously. I could be honest. Isn't honesty always the best policy?" she asked.

"Well, yes, most of the time. But sometimes in investigations, it doesn't work as well. What are you thinking?"

"I could say that I'm investigating a tour company who may have committed corporate espionage and stolen intellectual property from them. I could say I need to talk to the owner to work out a settlement with the estate of the recently deceased owner of the company in possession of the stolen said intellectual property," she said.

"Unbelievable," Alen said again. "But what if they say okay. Then you're opening up Kaylee's company to an investigation," he warned.

"That's where the role play comes in. I don't have to use my real name or Kaylee's name or the company name. I don't even have to say I'm in Italy. I could be calling from Texas, U.S.A. because if the phone system logs numbers that's the area code and exchange for my U.S. digital number," she said, jotting down notes.

"Unbelievable and brilliant too," Alen exclaimed. He was proud of her.

"I think it will sound more professional and more believable instead of asking to talk to the owner to ask for the owner's name and contact information. Do you agree?"

"I do," he said. "And if you hurry, you have time to call before dinner is ready."

She dialed the number from the website listing.

"Hello, I'm trying to reach Matthew McKenzie, please," Joan said into her phone.

"Yes, ma'am. My name is Taly Atwater," she said.

"Of course, I'll hold," she looked at Alen wide-eyed and mouthed, she's connecting me.

"Mr. McKenzie, good afternoon. My name is Taly Atwater, and I'm an investigative journalist. Through research I discovered that Great Pond Logistics is the parent company of the WiseTours app, is that right?"

## Victimized in Venice

"Oh, no, sir, there is no problem with your app. I was doing a documentary on a tour company after the owner died mysteriously, and I believe I discovered that the company plagiarized some of your tour material. I was wondering if you could share the owner's contact information with me that I could pass on to the attorney handling the estate for the deceased owner so a settlement could be reached. I think it's only fair you be compensated. That is called corporate espionage or theft of intellectual property. Since the owner is dead, there's no reason to seek legal action, but I believe the company wants to make some restitution. And of course, they will agree to stop using the material," she explained and then took a deep but silent breath.

Alen looked on amazed.

"I see. Yes, sir, I understand. Do you have a legal department?...Oh, right. Yes, I'm happy to give you my contact information. Taly Atwater, 361-555-7136. Thank you very much, you have a good afternoon too."

"Well, tell me, what did he say?" Alen asked.

"Reading between the lines, I just stirred a big ole Texas-sized hornet's nest," she said.

"Why? What did he say?"

"He said he and his fiancée are the owners of Great Pond Logistics. It's a small company. They have no legal department. In fact, they have no departments at all. He creates phone apps, his fiancée runs the business. She also owns a tour company, but she's currently living in Italy. He'll tell her to call me,"

"Oh no, do you think..." Alen started to say. Joan was nodding her head.

"I think we found Kaylee's boyfriend, who likely doesn't know she's dead. And it appears her family knows nothing about him or her secondary company. You were right, she didn't have time to do the paperwork for My Venice, because she was already running another company. Someone has to tell that man she's dead. But I don't want to tell him over the phone," she said.

"We have some time to think about this. You handled that so well, Sweetheart. I'm so proud of you," he said and kissed her. "I know the timing isn't the best but dinner's ready. What do you say, we try to forget all this for just tonight. We both need to relax. Tomorrow is soon enough to figure this all out," Alen said.

"I can't wait to try your Barbecue Chicken Spaghetti, finally!"

## Chapter Seventeen

JOAN AND ALEN WERE SHOCKED when they went out to take Carina for her morning walk. Alen promised her they would only walk Carina together until they could figure out what was going on with the Casanova dude. The morning seemed perfectly normal. They got dressed, put Carina's leash on her and rode the elevator done to the first floor.

The guard was at the desk, just like always. But when they exited the building, they thought they were on a movie set. They looked around and noted how quiet it was and proceeded on their way to Carina's favorite spot, the park.

No people were walking in the neighborhood. Joan could see only three supply boats on the canal where usually there were dozens.

"What happened? Where is everyone?" she asked.

"It feels like the city was evacuated and we missed it or something. I think we better start checking the news more often or something," Alen said.

Joan shivered as a chill washed over her. She hoped Alen was wrong and they didn't sleep through a city-wide evacuation. The feeling was creepy.

They took Carina to the park and encouraged her to do her business quickly.

"While we're here, I want you to show me the gate you went through following Casanova last night. I was going to ask last night, but we were tired and I decided in the daylight would be better," he said.

Joan was trying not to be scared and wanted to go back home. But she knew Alen, and she was certain he was not going to rest until he scoped this out.

"It's over here," she said, leading the way to the tree-covered walkway.

Alen looked high and low as well as on both sides of the walkway on the way to the gate that led to the alley.

"What are you looking for?" Joan asked.

"Anything. Maybe something fell off his costume. A wrapper or piece of paper he dropped. Anything that could be evidence should we ever need it," he said.

They walked through the iron gate. Joan noticed that it creaked when Alen pulled it open. She had not noticed that yesterday. This morning felt so quiet. She realized she was listening for a buzz that she heard yesterday. As she listened, she realized the noise from the day before was in her head. It wasn't from a machine or an exterior source. It was from adrenaline rushing through her body.

"You went straight to the end? You didn't take either of these turns, right?" Alen asked her as they walked passed the little café table outside the hotel entrance.

"No. I stopped at this table on my way back and talked to an older couple. They weren't sitting there when we went by the first time," she recalled for him.

## Victimized in Venice

They reached the end of the alley. Joan freaked out. The busy concourse lined with businesses was devoid of crowds of people.

"There were hundreds of people walking this plaza yesterday. I couldn't even see the other side for all the people! Where is everyone?" she asked, not expecting an answer.

"Joan, Sweetheart, it's only seven-thirty in the morning. It might be eight by now. I'm sure these businesses are never open this early and it's not time yet for the usual heavy traffic," he reminded her.

"Oh, I feel silly and stupid. Why am I so freaked out?"

"There are fewer people than normal in the park, and there aren't as many boats on the water. I do think something is different. But it's not as bad as all that, at least I hope not. Let's go see if our regular breakfast café is open. That will tell us something either way," he said comforting her.

"Thanks. You're right. That's a great idea."

They walked back down the alley, through the iron gate to the park and on their normal route home. Their breakfast café was open, but there was not a line to get their coffee and brioche.

"*Ciao*, Henry," Joan greeted the morning barista who they learned spoke English.

"*Ciao,* Signore Joan e Signore Alen. Your usual this morning?" Henry inquired.

"Yes, please, Henry," Alen said.

"Henry, where are all the people?" Joan asked.

"They are home. Probably where we should be too. But I have to open for my customers. The news this morning is grave. There are hundreds now infected with the coronavirus. Some in Venice too. The virus is highly contagious and can be very dangerous for some people. The government is trying to stop the spread. They want everyone to stay home. Do you have food at home for a few days at least?"

"Yes, we do. We'll be fine. You take care, Henry. We're going home to read the news. We'll still be walking Carina three times a day, we will stop in more often to see you," Joan promised.

When they got back to the penthouse, they discovered they had an email from Holly and Ray. They were afraid, if they waited any longer to return, they might be refused entry. The email assured Alen and Joan they were welcome to stay at the penthouse for as long as they needed to stay, but they would be home the following day.

Alen took an inventory of groceries in the kitchen while Joan read the news articles about the virus aloud.

"I'm going to draw up some meal plans for the four of us and make a trip to the grocery store to stock up for a while," Alen said.

"I'm going to message the homeowners for our next house sitting job and see what's going on there and if they are considering canceling their trip. Then I'm going to clean the house for Ray and Holly's return. But before they get back, we need to figure out how to tell poor Matthew McKenzie that his fiancée is dead," she said.

"First, we need to verify that Kaylee is his fiancée," Alen reminded her.

"Yeah, it would be too freaky if there was another American here who owned a tour company that used the same canned descriptions, but it is possible, I suppose and you're right. We do need to verify that before we say, hey, your future wife is gone. I don't know which is worse, to hear that about the woman you love, or to find out your woman is okay after all, it was someone else who died. Sheesh, what a mess," Joan said.

"I can't figure out why no one knew if she had a boyfriend or was engaged, and how was she engaged to someone who lives in the U.S. when she was here?"

"Online dating? Maybe he traveled here. Maybe she took trips there. We don't know much about her life at all," she answered.

~***~

Late that afternoon, Alen and Joan decided to call Lesley and inquire about Kaylee's life before they made the call to Matthew McKenzie. They didn't want to be the ones to tell her family that Kaylee was engaged, and they didn't want to have to tell the fiance that his betrothed was gone. But they agreed that the later was better than the former. At least, that's how it felt at the time.

"Hi, Lesley, it's Joan. How are you all? Is everyone okay?"

"Hi, Joan, yes, we're all fine. I'm sure it will get old soon, but for today, we are enjoying the forced break and day home with family. Are you guys okay?"

"Yes, we're good. I'm sure you know Holly and Ray will be back tomorrow. Alen went and stocked up on groceries this afternoon, and I cleaned house. At least the grocery stores were still open. He said it felt like an abandoned apocalyptic town until he got there and he said he found everyone," they both laughed.

"Neither of you has any symptoms, do you?"

"No, no, we're fine," Joan said

"I'm worried about Holly and Ray flying back, but at least there haven't been many cases in the U.S. yet."

"True. Listen, I called because I wondered if we could talk a little bit about Kaylee. Would that be too painful for you?" Joan asked.

"I would like that, I think. What do you want to talk about?" Lesley asked.

"I feel like it's too soon to talk to Ray or Zach about her, but I wondered what her life was like here. Did she date?"

"Not that she ever talked about. Zach used to tease her about it. He would say, Kay, you gotta find someone to love besides your reflection. They would laugh. She had a great sense of humor with him, just not many other people. He would say, I don't care if you find a man, a woman, an alien, I just want you to have love in your life. But no animals. Beastiality is not cool. I think if she ever dated someone, she would have told him even if no one else.," she answered.

"Did she travel much?" Joan asked.

"Every three months or so she would say she had to get out of town. I need a breather, she would say. Sometimes she would go to Paris, but most of the time I think she stayed in Italy. She would go to

Milan, Rome, Florence, Tuscany. She said sometimes she just needed to walk on solid ground," Lesley said.

"I understand that. I already had the feeling that I want to walk on solid ground, drive a car. Ride on a street. Did Zoe or her other friends travel with her?"

"No, those were her getaways. She always went alone. Kaylee was the quintessential introvert. She enjoyed her own company better than the company of anyone else," Lesley said.

"I hope this doesn't sound judgemental because I don't mean it that way at all. I'm just curious. Her friends gave the tours, she only worked the tours if someone was sick, and you did all the paperwork. She wasn't in school. She wasn't dating. Ray mentioned she never had the time to spend with him and Holly. What did she do all day?"

"I used to wonder that too. She did set up the marketing with the cruise ship companies. She orchestrated getting the printed materials made and distributed to them too. She said she went to the gym, and she did research about the buildings here, the histories. She said she was working on some new tour ideas with legends. She wanted to offer something edgier. But I used to wonder, I take care of two preschoolers, a house, a husband, and all her business accounting. It seemed like she should have hours free every day. But she never mentioned what she did with her time," Lesley said.

"Interesting. Do you know if she was working with anyone else about the new tour ideas? Did she share any of that with you, or is it all lost now?" Joan asked hoping she wasn't pushing too much.

"Not that I know of. She never mentioned anyone. We have to clean out her apartment before the end of the month. I'm going to help Holly, and we're going to pack everything up so Ray and Zach don't have to do it. I'm hoping I find notes, or there is stuff on her computer or something. If not, it is all lost," Lesley said.

"Thanks for answering my questions. I know it's really none of our business. We're starting to feel like we know her, and I couldn't picture what her life was like here," Joan said.

"No, you guys have helped so much in so many ways. We appreciate it. Kaylee has always been a big mystery, and now, it seems, she always will be one," Lesley said.

They ended their call, and Joan relayed Lesley's side of the call to Alen.

"So it's possible she was meeting with Matthew when she traveled. And it's also possible that he even came here. Her life was secluded and private. If no one saw her for a few days, no one would think anything of it, right?"

"That's what I'm thinking. Holly and Lesley are going to pack up her apartment. I wonder what they will find."

"I guess we have to call Matthew. Do you want me to do it?"

"Yes, if you feel up to it. I've not ever had to be the person who told someone their loved one died. I'm not ready for that," she explained. "Besides, he knows my voice as Taly Atwater, Texas investigative reporter. It feels beyond wrong to tell him using that persona," she said.

"I meant to ask you where you came up with that name," Alen said.

"I was considering an anagram of Italy. Taly popped into my head. Almost pig Latin for Italy, but when I thought of Taly, I remember the character for a favorite movie, Up Close and Personal. Michelle Pfeiffer plays a want-to-be reporter named Tally Atwater. They made her change her stage name to Sally, but that's where it came from. I figured a young man wouldn't have seen the movie, and if he was old and his wife made him watch the movie with her, he would have either slept through it or forgotten. It's a chick flick."

"Woman, you amaze me," he said fondly. "How about making us some coffee? I'll call young Matthew, verify he was in love with Kaylee, and break the news to him. Then we can walk Carina, and if the café is open, we'll get something to eat. I have a feeling we are going to be stuck in the house for the foreseeable future."

"Okay, I like that plan. Do you want me to bring you a cup of coffee when it's ready?"

"No, I'll come and get it when I'm done. This call might be brutal. You don't need to have to hear it."

~***~

Alen confirmed what Joan feared. Matthew was Kaylee's fiancé, he came to Italy every three months and they would travel together. He was devastated and heartbroken to learn she was gone. Alen learned he was in Italy the week before Kaylee died. They argued. She wanted to go back to the United States. He wanted her to stay in Italy and was planning to join her within the next six months. He was getting all of his paperwork ready to emigrate. He explained to Alen that he tried to reason with her that there was much more money to be made in Europe than in the U.S. Kaylee never told Matthew she had family in Venice. She said she was estranged from her family, that it was painful, and he never questioned her about it.

And Alen was right about what the next few days would look like in Venice. Virtually everything was shut down. The white tablecloth adorned tables in San Marco Plaza sat vacant. Museums and attractions were closed. Joan helped Holly and Lesley pack up Kaylee's apartment, and other than walking Carina, they stayed home to avoid the virus. They played cards together, Holly and Alen took turns cooking, and they read novels. Joan and Alen were determined to find something to do to make Valentine's Day special in Venice. Their next house sitting job was still on track, but Joan had her heart set on attending Zoe's wedding and they stayed in Venice.

Lesley took Kaylee's computer home to see if there was any information on it about the tours she wanted to develop. She promised to let them know if she found anything interesting.

At night, in their room, Joan and Alen would quietly discuss Kaylee's murder and rehashed every conversation looking for something they missed. Scouring the city for new suspects wasn't a possibility. They still wanted to solve the murder. And as long as they were in Venice, they vowed there was still a chance they would.

# Chapter Eighteen

VALENTINE'S DAY MORNING, JOAN AWOKE to the smell of freshly brewed coffee and her husband standing next to the bed with a tray.

"Good morning, handsome. Whatcha got there on that tray? Do I smell coffee?"

"You are a talented sleuth, my love. Happy Valentine's Day!" he said.

Joan sat up against the headboard and Alen placed the lap tray in front of her. There was indeed coffee, and fresh croissants from Henry's café, still warm with strawberry butter and fresh fruit for two. Alen sat down on his side of the bed.

"Happy Valentine's Day, Honey. Oh, these croissants are still warm. Thank you. What time is it? Did I oversleep?"

"No, you slept just right. Henry and I had an appointment early this morning. Holly and Ray just left with Carina. When they get back, we'll pick out our costumes for the day," he said.

"I'm so excited about this wedding. And I'm glad Holly and Ray are back to attend the special day too. Zoe was Kaylee's best friend, and I think being close to her helps Ray. I anticipate she will become like an adopted daughter to them," Joan said.

"So, my favorite bride, you have the morning plans. What are we doing this morning?"

"We're taking a gondola ride first to the island of Burano. Our private tour guide, Blake, will lead us on a strolling tour of the most colorful island in Venice. We will dine on a four-star lunch at *Trattoria al Gatto Nego*, the Black Cat Tavern, and then we'll go to the island of Murano where we can watch them create the most beautiful hand-blown glass in the world, often used to make jewelry. It shouldn't be crowded or too peopley but I'm hoping for pretty weather," she said.

"That sounds like a perfect morning," Alen said. "And I believe we are both in luck because the sun was just beginning its ascent when I was walking back from Henry's and I couldn't find a single cloud in the sky. Then we'll go to the wedding, right?"

"Right. And after the wedding, it is all up to you. How will we spend the end of the day?"

"I wasn't sure how the wedding was going to go and how long we would want to stay there. So I wanted to be flexible," he said.

"Alen! Are you using the wedding to get out of making plans? That's not like you at all," she scolded.

"Of course not! This is the second most important day of the year. The day I celebrate the love of my life. My traveling companion and tour guide. You do a wonderful job of scheduling activities. But if we've learned nothing at all since we started house sitting, we should have learned to be flexible. That's all I was saying. I do have plans, and destinations in mind. But I'm keeping it a surprise. There is no sense in rushing through the day. We should cherish every moment of this day, our last full day in Venice and it will be spectacular," Alen promised.

## Victimized in Venice

Joan still was skeptical about whether he had real plans or not, but it didn't matter. They were together, they were getting out of the house, and it would be fun.

Before Holly and Ray left, when they tried on costumes, Joan and Alen had selected coordinating red and gold jester costumes from the Roberts' collection to wear for Carnival. But since they were attending the wedding, the couple opted for a more formal set. Holly assured them they should select the costumes they liked best because she and Ray liked them all and it didn't matter to them which ones they wore to the wedding.

They selected an ice blue and ecru set of 18$^{th}$-century finery. The costumes were heavy, the hats tall, and the masks full. There were no wigs, but the costume included a smooth hood that flowed from the bodices over the hair and under the hat, so no hair was exposed eliminating the need for wigs. There was a matching satin drawstring back with a wrist band where Joan could carry their identification, money for the day and the envelope that contained their wedding gift to Zoe and Fabio, a cash contribution in the Italian tradition of 500 euros from them both, in a card. Holly had told Joan that Zoe would have a pouch, not unlike the one Joan would be carrying where guests would drop their gift.

Fabio's father, the atelier, had come to their rescue the day before and delivered period shoes to the penthouse for them to rent for the day.

While Alen and Joan were in their room giggling and laughing while trying to sort out all the various pieces of the costumes and get dressed, they received an unexpected phone call.

"Hello, Lesley. Happy Valentine's Day," Joan said when she answered.

"Hi, Happy Valentine's Day to you too. I know you guys have big plans for the day, but I have to tell you something. I found something on Kaylee's computer, and I don't know what to do about it. Or with it. Or anything," Lesley said.

In her corset and petticoat, Joan sat down on the side of the bed and gave Lesley her full attention.

"I'm listening," Joan said into the phone, "I'm putting you on speaker so Alen can hear too."

"No, don't!" Lesley pleaded.

"Okay. I won't, what's wrong?"

"I'm sorry, I don't mind if Alen hears this, I just don't know where you are and I don't want Ray or Holly to hear it," Lesley explained.

"I understand. I don't have you on speaker. We are in our bedroom getting dressed. I don't know where anyone else is in the house. But you're safe. Tell me, what did you find?"

"Kaylee did have a boyfriend. His name was Matthew and they were engaged!" Lesley said.

"I know," Joan said without thinking.

"You know? How do you know?" Lesley asked.

"We ran across him in our investigation. I'm sorry. I knew from talking to you and her friends that for some reason Kaylee was keeping Matthew a secret. We didn't think it was our secret to tell, so we didn't say anything," Joan explained.

"Did you also know that she owned another company with him?" Lesley asked.

"Um, yes. I'm sorry. That's actually how we found Matthew. Alen and I had taken one of the self-guided tours when we first got here. The day we each took a tour, we recognized that the tour guides were using the same information. We thought Kaylee had adopted another company's verbiage and that might have angered someone enough to kill her. So, we dug trying to find the owner of that company, and that's how we learned about Matthew. He was listed as the contact on Great Pond Logistic's BBB membership roster," Joan explained.

"Wow. Is there anything else you know that we should know?" Lesley asked.

## Victimized in Venice

Her tone was even, but Joan couldn't decide if the words were meant to bite.

"I don't think so. I'm sorry if you feel betrayed. We did what we thought was best," Joan said.

"No, not at all. I understand. That's why I didn't want to be on the speaker. I can't decide whether to tell Zach and Ray or not, and I won't say anything to Holly until I decide, because that would just put her in the same predicament you and I are in. It helps to talk about it. I won't take up any more of your time. Enjoy your day. We'll see you at the wedding. I hope you have some time tomorrow before you leave that we can talk?" Lesley asked hopefully.

"I'll make sure we have some time tomorrow. See you later," Joan said before disconnecting.

~***~

The gondola ride was wonderful. They happened to get one of the gondoliers who enjoyed singing for his passengers. Joan had learned early in their stay that not all gondoliers sang and many hated being asked. This one was in the spirit of the day, spoke English, and regaled them with That's Amore, as made famous by Dean Martin. But he sang it in English on the way to Burano and in Italian on the trip to Murano.

They shared a plate of *spaghetti alla busara,* or spaghetti with prawns. The chef came out and talked with Alen about cooking and then served them clementine-scented marzipan biscuits for dessert.

They had forty-five minutes to wander the streets of Murano before they needed to arrive at the glass cathedral. Many of the glassblowing shops were closed, though a few were open. Joan had hoped to see at least one of the artisans at work, but window shopping was almost as much fun, walking hand in hand with Alen.

When they arrived at the Glass Cathedral, Joan and Alen, as well as the other guests were delighted to see three glassblowers entertaining in the lobby. Not only was the glass beautiful, but these three had also perfected the art of entertaining.

"This may upstage the wedding," Alen said.

"I know. All the guests are out here and it seems everyone is reluctant to leave," Joan agreed.

The artisans completed their art and their act. To everyone's surprise, the bride appeared. She was wearing an exquisite and elaborate 18th-century wedding dress. And it turned out she was part of the performance.

The three glassblowers kneeled before the bride, each on one knee. Each one held a velvet pillow with their piece of glasswork jewelry upon the pillow. The guests had witnessed the creation of Zoe's wedding jewels. One glassblower offered a necklace, another a bracelet, and the third a glass flower the bride would carry instead of a bouquet. Miraculously, all of the pieces matched perfectly, demonstrating the skill the artisans possessed to create the same patterns while dancing and twirling around entertaining the audience. The crowd burst into applause. The glassblowers stood and bowed to Zoe, turned and bowed to the audience and then left the lobby. The guests were then directed to the room where the wedding would take place. The crowd poured into a beautiful room where the wedding would take place.

"When I heard the name the Glass Cathedral, I expected it to be made of glass," Alen said.

"Me too" Joan whispered.

They spotted Holly and Ray and took seats next to them. A moment later Lesley, Zach, and their girls Avery and Brenna, who were darling and looked like tiny princesses, joined them.

While they waited for the ceremony to begin, Joan studied the glass chandeliers made from the magical Murano glass. She decided it was a perfect place for a wedding.

And then she spotted him. She gasped. Alen heard her and looked at her to see what startled her. He followed her gaze and just before he realized what she was looking at, she said, "Call the police, Alen, call the police. Hurry."

## Victimized in Venice

Alen didn't hesitate, he pulled out his phone and dialed the number for the police in Italy, 112. He started to stand up and Joan pulled him back down to his seat. The wedding was about to start and she didn't want to create a scene, even though Casanova, her Casanova, was standing at the wedding altar with the groom.

Alen whispered into the phone, "We need the police at Glass Cathedral and he prayed the person on the other end could hear him and understand him. He couldn't recall at the moment how to say Glass Cathedral in Italian.

"I understand, signore. I send police to Santa Chiara Murano. Do you need to stay on the call with me? Are you in danger?"

"No. I'm at a wedding, and I believe there is a murderer here," he said and disconnected the call. He reached for Joan's hand and squeezed it tightly. She stared at the man and prayed the police arrived soon.

The music was playing, the groom and his best man stood at the front of the room and everyone waited for the bride. Doors at the back of the room burst open. It wasn't the bride who came through them though. It was the police.

"Alen, how did they get here that quick?" Joan whispered.

"Beats me. But I think they were already here," he answered as everyone gaped and wondered what was happening.

Two officers reached Casanova and arrested him. Joan recognized Ispettore Capo Pula from the night the police came to the penthouse. She was the female officer who spoke English. She spoke to the groom who then rushed to the back of the room and out through the doors, and then she stood bravely in front of the room to make an announcement.

When she spoke in Italian her words caused a collective gasp in the crowd and then a bevy of hushed whispers and chatter in Italian. The English speakers all wondered what was happening. Lesley and Zach understood the Italian and sat speechless staring at the officer.

Finally, she began to say something in English. Joan and Alen understood why the crowd reacted because they were shocked too.

"I'm sorry to inform you, but there will be no wedding today. The bride, Zoe Lee and her brother, Matt Lee, are under arrest for the charge of murder. The hosts invite you to please enjoy the refreshments before you leave."

Zach looked at Ray and said, "I'm going to try to get more answers. I'll be back," and he followed Fabio's path out the back of the wedding room and through the doors in search of police officers who would or could tell him if this had anything to do with his sister.

People began to file out of the room. Some left the cathedral. Others went to the room next door where the meal was to take place. Still, others milled around the lobby where just moments before the glassblowers performed.

The American group stood together in the lobby waiting for Zach to return with information.

Waiters were circulating the room distributing glasses of Prosecco and treats that Joan and Alen learned were called Gondola kisses. The kisses reminded Joan of the chocolates from back home called Kisses. They were two meringues with the flat sides stuck together with a creamy chocolate filling. Each outer side had the shape of the familiar chocolate Kisses.

Small children were passing out fabric bags to the guests. Lesley explained the bags were called *bomboniere* and were gifts for the guests. She explained that the bags contained *confetti*, not colorful shapes of paper to throw and the wedding couple, but candied almonds.

"It still amazes me how many traditions are the same all over the world," Alen said.

"I agree. I can't wait to find out what happened. Do you think this could have anything to do with Kaylee? Zoe was her best friend!" Lesley asked. She had one little girl holding each of her hands. The girls, not understanding what was happening, were chattering to each other and trying to dance in their pretty princess gowns despite the tight grip their mother had on them.

Ray saw Zach first. He was looking around the room trying to find them. Ray waved at him.

Zach pointed to the now empty wedding room and they all understood. They returned to the empty quiet room for him to tell them what was happening. Lesley wisely sent the girls to the front of the room to dance so they wouldn't hear what their father had to say.

"Wow, this is so surreal," Zach started. "Zoe and her brother, Matthew, were just arrested for Kaylee's death. The polizia have thought all along the killer was a woman from the bruises on Kaylee's neck. They found fingerprints at Kaylee's apartment that matched Zoe's brother's on file with immigration. But Alen and Joan, the tip you gave me about Lapo Muni was the one that solved the case. I didn't catch it, but the Inspettore Superiore who delivered the news to us about Kaylee was also named Muni. When I called with the tip about Lapo, it was his cousin. The detective knew how to find Lapo. When he did, he found out that Lapo saw Zoe, who he recognized, and a man he didn't recognize dragging the duffel bag with the body and dumping it in the river. He didn't know Kaylee was in it but had decided he didn't like living in Venice and moved to Amalfi. When they confronted Zoe, she confessed and told them her brother helped her dispose of the body." Zach paused.

"But why? Why did she kill Kaylee?" an anguished Ray asked.

"As we all now know, Zoe and Fabio kept their relationship and engagement a secret because Kaylee had forbidden Zoe to date the Italian if she wanted to keep her job. Zoe kept it a secret while she trained to become a licensed guide and secured a job with the company that Fabio worked for. She went to Kaylee's that night to confess the engagement and resign from her job. But when she got there, Kaylee told her she was engaged to a secret boyfriend. Zoe snapped. She reached for Kaylee's neck, squeezed and shook her. She didn't mean to kill her, but the rage and adrenaline took over and it happened. She panicked and called her brother Matt, who devised the plan to dump her in the canal," Zach finished.

"Kaylee was engaged? To who? Did you know about this?" Ray asked Zach.

"I didn't know," Zach said.

"She was engaged to a man named Matthew McKenzie in the United States. He was working on moving here to be with her," Lesley said.

Zach looked at her stunned, "You knew about this? And you didn't tell me?"

"I just found it this morning going through her computer. It took me a few days of searching through papers to find her email password and then I found their emails and online chats. I didn't know whether to say anything or not. I don't understand why she was keeping it a secret," Lesley said.

"That's a mystery we may never solve. But I would like to meet this man. Do you know how to get in touch with him?" Ray asked.

"We do," Alen said. "Joan and I talked to him while we were investigating. He's a nice young man who is devastated with grief. I'm sure he would like to meet you too, we have his contact information at the penthouse."

"Thank you. Thank you to you both. Without you we might never have learned what happened to my daughter," Ray said. He took Holly's hand and walked out of the cathedral.

Zach and Lesley gathered the tiny princesses and left too. Alen and Joan were alone in the room.

"This was going to be a beautiful wedding," Joan muttered while sitting down on one of the benches. Alen looked at his wife. It was just six days until their anniversary. He realized he loved her, even more, today than on their wedding day.

He took her hand, pulled her up from her seat and looped her arm through his. He then walked her up to the front of the altar, turned and faced her.

## Victimized in Venice

"My beautiful, Joan, the best decision I ever made was donating hundreds of dollars to the 9/11 Memorial Fund," he said referring to how they met. Joan laughed. Because it was a funny story and an even funnier memory.

"My second best decision was asking you to marry me. And my third best decision was agreeing to this crazy life of being house sitters. I love you more today than any other day. I love that you make me laugh, I love that you don't let me get too serious about myself, and I love that you always surprise me. Thank you for being my wife, and if I had it to do all over again, I would only change one thing. I would have done it sooner," he said. He then kissed her.

"My handsome Alen, I love you too, but if I had it to do all over again, I would have you wearing that sexy apron with a kilt instead of these hot, heavy, itchy costumes," she said and they both laughed.

"Seriously, there is no one I would rather spend my days with. Thank you for this day. It's beautiful and will be an everlasting memory in our collection of special days together." she said.

Alen reached inside his coat pocket and pulled out a small gift box. He handed the box to Joan. She opened it carefully, certain she already knew what the box contained. It was a silver charm for her bracelet he started for her in Edinburgh and the charm was a gondola.

Joan opened the drawstring closed pouch hanging from her wrist and withdrew a small envelope. She handed it to Alen.

"What's this?" he asked surprised.

"You gave me a gift. I need to give you one," she said. "Actually, your Valentine's gift is at the penthouse. I couldn't carry it around all day. This is the 500 euros we thought we were spending on a wedding gift today."

"Woohoo, we're rich!" he said. "Whadda say we blow this joint. I'm starving!"

"How can you be starving? We just had lunch?" she asked as they left the cathedral in search of a gondola to take them back to Venice.

"I just don't think I've said that in a while and it seemed appropriate," he said.

"It was. So, was that surprise vow renewal back there your plan for the day?" Joan asked.

"No, that was completely spontaneous. I was moved by the location and opportunity. Now, I will begin to try to woo my bride in the city of love."

~***~

Lesley, Zach, Brenna, and Avery came to the penthouse to see Joan and Alen off. Along with Holly and Ray, they felt like Alen and Joan were part of the family now.

"Thank you for everything," Ray said emotionally. "Matthew is on his way to Venice. We are going to have a memorial for Kaylee here. We want to hear about the Kaylee he knew and fell in love with. Then we'll send her back to the United States where she was the happiest."

"I'm taking over the Italy company with Fabio and Leah as you know, but I've also agreed to help Matthew with the financials for Great Pond Logistics. It's been so nice getting to know you guys," Lesley said.

"I received the notification that you guys joined the Patreon initiative to help with the affordable housing project here, thank you," Zach said.

"Hey, you never said, where are you going next?" Holly asked.

"Ensenada, Mexico," Joan said.

"Travel safely and may you always be one step ahead of the virus," Ray said.

"Bon voyage!" they all said as Alen and Joan stepped into the elevator.

They heard a bark and a scrambling of toenails. Alen pushed the door open button in the elevator, and Joan crouched to receive a parting hug from Carina.

*To be continued…*

## A message from Scarlett:

Hello, I know you have over a million choices of books to read. I can't tell you how much it means to me that you chose to spend some of your limited and valued reading time reading one of my books.

I truly appreciate it and hope I entertained you. If I did, I would appreciate a few more minutes of your time, if I may humbly ask, for you to leave a review for other readers who might be trying to select their next reading material.

If for any reason you were not satisfied with this book, let me know how I can do better by emailing me directly at scarlett.moss@scarlettbraden.com.

The satisfaction of my readers and your feedback is important to me.

Hugs from Ecuador,
Scarlett

Sign up for the cozy mystery newsletter to be informed when new books are released or sales are going on here:

bit.ly/CozyNewsletter

SCARLETT MOSS

# The House Sitters Cozy Mysteries:

How it all began is featured in the Prequel: Corrupted in Corpus Christi. And you can get it free by signing up for Scarlett's Cozy Mysteries Newsletter! Here's the link to sign up: Scarlett's Newsletter

If you don't want to receive the newsletter or you prefer a paperback, you can purchase it wherever books are sold online. It's available in eBook, Paperback, and Large Print.

books2read.com/u/49QrN0

Other books in the House Sitter series:
#1 Exposed in Edinburgh:
https://www.amazon.com/dp/B0836DZKS9
#2 Leveled in London:
https://www.amazon.com/dp/B083Y6CKFP
#3 Victimized in Venice (3-17-2020):
https://www.amazon.com/dp/B084WLGR2S

Coming Soon #4

Erased in Ensenada

# About the Author

Scarlett Moss is a pen name for Scarlett Braden's cozy mystery books. Scarlett also writes thrillers and poetry.

Originally from the southern United States, Scarlett now calls the Andes mountains of Ecuador home. She lives there with her husband and her Ecuadorian pound puppy, Picasso.

Scarlett found her writing voice and her passion for writing late in life and now it's her favorite thing to do, usually with Picasso, the writer's assistant, by her side or in her lap. She also enjoys the festivals and holidays of her adopted country.

If you would like to hang out with Scarlett, she would love to have you in her Facebook readers group called Scarlett's Cozy Couch: where you can get to know her better, enjoy her twisted sense of humor, and sometimes even win prizes. You can join here: https://www.facebook.com/groups/ScarlettsSafeRoom/

If you just want to lurk and follow the progress of her cozy mystery books, you can follow the Scarlett Moss Facebook page here: https://www.facebook.com/ScarlettMossMysteries

Sign up for the cozy mystery newsletter to be informed when new books are released or sales are going on here: bit.ly/CozyNewsletter

SCARLETT MOSS

Printed in Great Britain
by Amazon